YEARLING BOOKS/YOUNG YEARLINGS/YEARLING CLASSICS are designed especially to entertain and enlighten young people. Patricia Reilly Giff, consultant to this series, received the bachelor's degree from Marymount College. She holds the master's degree in history from St. John's University, and a Professional Diploma in Reading from Hofstra University. She was a teacher and reading consultant for many years, and is the author of numerous books for young readers.

For a complete listing of all Yearling titles, write to
Dell Readers Service, P.O. Box 1045,
South Holland, IL 60473.

BEVERLY CLEARY

RAMONA FOREVER

ILLUSTRATED BY ALAN TIEGREEN

A YEARLING BOOK

Published by
Dell Publishing
a division of
The Bantam Doubleday Dell Publishing Group, Inc.
666 Fifth Avenue
New York, New York 10103

The trademark Yearling® is registered in the U.S. Patent and Trademark office.

ISBN: 0-440-47243-1

Reprinted by arrangement with William Morrow and Company, Inc.

Printed in the United States of America

One Previous Edition

September 1988

20   19   18   17   16   15

CW

Contents

ONE

The Rich Uncle

"Guess what?" Ramona Quimby asked one Friday evening when her Aunt Beatrice dropped by to show off her new ski clothes and to stay for supper. Ramona's mother, father, and big sister Beezus, whose real name was Beatrice, paid no attention and went on eating. Picky-picky, the cat, meowed through the basement door, asking to share the meal.

Aunt Beatrice, who taught third grade, knew how to behave toward her third-grade niece.

1

"What?" she asked, laying down her fork as if she expected to be astounded by Ramona's news.

Ramona took a deep breath and announced, "Howie Kemp's rich uncle is coming to visit." Except for Aunt Bea, her family was not as curious as Ramona had hoped. She plunged on anyway because she was happy for her friend. "Howie's grandmother is really excited, and so are Howie and Willa Jean." And so, to be truthful, was Ramona, who disliked having to go to the Kemps' house after school, where Howie's grandmother looked after her grandchildren and Ramona while the two mothers were at work. A rich uncle, even someone else's rich uncle, should make those long after-school hours more interesting.

"I didn't know Howie had a rich uncle," said Mrs. Quimby.

"He's Howie's father's little brother, only now he's big," explained Ramona.

"Why, that must be Hobart Kemp," said

2

Aunt Beatrice. "He was in my class in high school."

"Oh, yes. I remember. That boy with the blond curly hair who played baseball." Mrs. Quimby motioned to her daughters to clear away the plates. "All the girls said he was cute."

"That's the one," said Aunt Bea. "He used to chew licorice and spit on the grass to make the principal think he was chewing tobacco like a professional baseball player, which was what he wanted to be."

"Where's this cute licorice-chewing uncle coming from, and how did he get so rich?" asked Ramona's father, beginning to be interested. "Playing baseball?"

"He's coming from—" Ramona frowned. "I can't remember the name, but it sounds like a fairy tale and has camels." Narnia? Never-never-land? No, those names weren't right.

"Saudi Arabia," said Beezus, who also went to the Kemps' after school. Being in junior high school, she could take her time getting there.

"Yes, that's it!" Ramona wished she had remembered first. "Howie says he's bringing the whole family presents." She imagined bags of gold like those in *The Arabian Nights*, which Beezus had read to her. Of course, nobody carried around bags of gold today, but she enjoyed imagining them.

"What's Howie's uncle doing in Saudi Arabia?" asked Mr. Quimby. "Besides spitting licorice in the sand?"

"Daddy, don't be silly," said Ramona. "I don't know exactly." Now that she was the center of attention, she wished she had more information. "Something about oil. Drills or rigs or something. Howie understands all about it. His uncle earned a lot of money." The Quimbys were a family who had to worry about money.

"Oh, that kind of rich," said Mr. Quimby. "I thought maybe a long-lost uncle had died and left him a castle full of servants, jewels, and rare old wines."

4

"Daddy, that's so old-fashioned," said Ramona. "That's only in books."

The conversation drifted off, leaving Ramona behind. Her father, who would earn his teaching credential in June, said he was inquiring around for schools that needed an art teacher, and he also told about the problems of the men who worked in the same frozen-food warehouse where he worked on weekends at below-freezing temperatures. Mrs. Quimby told about two people who got into an argument over a parking space at the doctor's office where she worked. Aunt Bea talked about a man named Michael who had invited her to go skiing and was the reason she had bought new ski clothes. Beezus wondered aloud if Michael would ask Aunt Bea to marry him. Aunt Bea laughed at that, saying she had known him only two weeks, but since this was January, there were several months of skiing left and there was no telling what might happen.

No more was said about Howie's uncle that

evening. Days went by. Uncle Hobart didn't come and didn't come. Every evening Mr. Quimby asked, "Has Old Moneybags arrived?" And Ramona had to say no.

Finally one morning, as Ramona and Howie were waiting for the school bus, Ramona said, "I don't think you have a rich uncle at all. I think you made him up."

Howie said he did too have a rich uncle. Even little Willa Jean, when Ramona went to the Kemps' after school, talked about Uncle Hobart and the presents he was bringing. Ramona informed Howie and Willa Jean rather crossly that her mother said it wasn't nice to talk about other people's money. They paid no attention—after all, he was their very own uncle, not Ramona's—and went right on talking about Uncle Hobart this and Uncle Hobart that. Uncle Hobart had landed in New York. He had actually telephoned, live and in person. Uncle Hobart was driving across the country. Uncle Hobart was delayed by a storm in the

Rockies. Ramona wished she had never heard of Uncle Hobart.

Then, one day after school, Ramona and Howie saw a muddy van parked on the Kemps' driveway.

"It's Uncle Hobart!" Howie shouted, and began to run.

Ramona took her time. Somehow she had expected Uncle Hobart to arrive in a long black limousine, not a muddy van. She followed Howie into the house, where the famous uncle turned out to be a medium-young man who had not shaved for several days and who was wearing old jeans and a faded T-shirt. He was holding Willa Jean on his lap. The warm, sweet smell of apple pie filled the air.

"Down you go, Doll," said Uncle Hobart, lifting Willa Jean to the floor and grabbing Howie in a bear hug. "How's my favorite nephew?" he asked, and held Howie off to look at him while Mrs. Kemp hovered and Willa Jean embraced her Uncle Hobart's knee.

7

Ramona was embarrassed. She felt she was
in the way because she was not related. She sat
down on a chair, opened a book, but did not
read. She studied Uncle Hobart, who didn't
look rich to her. He looked like a plain man—a
big disappointment.

Willa Jean let go of her uncle's knee. "See what Uncle Hobart brought us," she said, and pointed to a pair of objects that looked like two small sawhorses, each holding a red leather cushion. Willa Jean sat astride one. "Giddyup, you old camel," she said and informed Ramona, "This is my camel saddle."

"Hey, a camel saddle!" said Howie when he saw his present. He imitated Willa Jean. After a few more giddyups, there was nothing more to do with a camel saddle except sit on it.

Pooh, who wants a boring old camel saddle, Ramona wanted to say, at the same time wishing she had a saddle to sit on these winter days when she liked to read by the furnace outlet.

Finally Uncle Hobart noticed Ramona. "Well, who's this young lady?" he asked. "Howie, you didn't tell me you had a girlfriend."

Both Ramona and Howie turned red and somehow felt ashamed.

"Aw, that's just old Ramona," Howie muttered.

To Ramona's horror, Uncle Hobart began to strum an imaginary guitar and sing:

"Ramona, I hear the mission bells above.
Ramona, they're ringing out our song of love.
I press you, caress you,
And bless the day you taught me to care."

Ramona knew right then that she did not like Uncle Hobart and never would. She had heard that song before. When Grandpa Day lived in Portland, he used to sing it to tease her, too. "I'm not Howie's girlfriend," she said in her most grown-up manner. "I have to stay here until my mother is through work. It is"— could she get the words out right? —"strictly a business arrangement."

Uncle Hobart found this very funny, which made Ramona dislike him even more.

"Cut it out, Uncle Hobart," said Howie, a remark much appreciated by Ramona, who pretended to read her book while inside she churned with anger. She was *glad* she didn't

10

have an Uncle Hobart. She was *glad* she didn't have any uncles at all, just Aunt Beatrice, who never embarrassed children and who always came when the family needed her.

"Did you bring us any more presents?" asked Willa Jean.

"Willa Jean, that isn't nice," said Mrs. Kemp, smiling because she was so happy to have her youngest son home at last.

"Willa Jean, how did you guess?" asked Uncle Hobart. "Come on out to the van, and I'll show you."

"Me, too?" Howie quickly forgot his annoyance.

"Sure." As he went out the door, Uncle Hobart said, "It's great to be back in a country full of green grass and trees."

Ramona heard Howie ask, "What do camels eat if there isn't any grass?"

When they returned, Ramona lost her struggle to be interested in her book. Uncle Hobart was carrying a small accordion.

"Grandma, look!" Howie was wheeling what

appeared to be part of a bicycle. "It's a real unicycle!"

"Is it broken?" asked Willa Jean. "It has only one wheel."

"Hobart, whatever were you thinking of?" Mrs. Kemp frowned at the unicycle.

"I was thinking of the unicycle you wouldn't let me have when I was Howie's age," said Uncle Hobart. "Now, Mom, don't you worry about a thing. I'll help him. He's not going to break any bones." He set the accordion on the floor by Willa Jean. "And this is for you," he said.

Willa Jean eyed the accordion. "What does it do?" she asked.

"You can play music on it," answered her uncle. "It's a Viennese accordion. I bought it from one of the men I worked with and even learned to play it a little."

"Isn't that lovely, Willa Jean?" said Mrs. Kemp. "Your very own musical instrument. We'll put it away until you're old enough to learn to play it."

"No!" Willa Jean put on her stubborn look. "I want to play it now!"

Uncle Hobart took the accordion and began to play and sing:

"Ramona, I hear the mission bells above,
  Ramona, they're ringing out our song of love."

Ramona stared at her book as she thought mean, dark thoughts about Uncle Hobart. He stopped playing and said, "What's the matter, Ramona? Don't you like my music?"

"No." Ramona looked the uncle in the eye. "You're teasing. I don't like grown-ups who tease."

"Why, Ramona!" Mrs. Kemp was most disapproving. "That's no way to talk to Howie's uncle."

"Now, Mom, don't get excited," said Uncle Hobart. "Ramona has a point. I was teasing, but I'll reform. Okay, Ramona?"

"Okay," agreed Ramona, suspecting he might still be teasing.

"Uncle Hobart, Uncle Hobart, let me play it," begged Willa Jean.

The Uncle placed Willa Jean's hands through the straps at each end of the accordion. "You squeeze in and pull out while you press the little buttons," he explained.

Before he could give any more instructions, Howie grabbed his uncle by the hand and dragged him outdoors. Mrs. Kemp, sure that bones were about to be broken, followed. Ramona watched through the window. Uncle Hobart hopped on the unicycle and, waving to his audience, pedaled to the corner and back. "See, nothing to it," he said. "Once you know how."

"Hobart, where on earth did you learn to ride that thing?" his mother called out from the front steps.

"In college," answered her son. "Come on, Howie, it's your turn." Holding the unicycle upright with one hand, he helped Howie mount the seat over the single wheel. "Now pedal," he directed. Howie pedaled; the unicycle tipped forward, setting Howie on the sidewalk.

Indoors, Willa Jean struggled with the accordion, too heavy for her, and made it give out a loud groan, as if it were in pain.

"No, not that way," Ramona heard Uncle Hobart say. "It's like riding a bicycle, only instead of balancing sideways, you have to balance back and forth at the same time."

With a flushed and determined face, Howie mounted the unicycle again. If he learns to ride it, maybe he'll let me ride his bicycle, thought Ramona, who longed for a bicycle, even a secondhand, three-speed bicycle. Howie tipped over backward into his uncle's arms. The accordion squawked. Ramona felt rather lonely, left out and in the way.

"Hobart, do be careful," shouted Mrs. Kemp above the squawk and screech of Willa Jean's playing.

Ramona could see that learning to ride a unicycle was going to take time, so she turned her attention to Willa Jean and the accordion.

Willa Jean set her gift on the floor and sat down on her camel saddle with a scowl. "It's too big and it won't play music."

"Let me try." Ramona was sure she could make music come out of the accordion. It looked so easy. She slipped her hands through the straps. The only song she could think of was, unfortunately, "Ramona." She pumped and pushed the buttons, only to produce the cry of a suffering accordion. She tried pushing different buttons while she pushed the bellows in and out. *Hee-haw, hee-haw.* This was not the music Ramona had in mind. "Maybe your uncle can show you how when he has more time," she told Willa Jean as she set the accordion down carefully on Howie's camel saddle.

From outside, Mrs. Kemp's warnings continued. "Hobart! Howie! Be careful!"

Ramona and Willa Jean stood by the window to watch Howie, protected by his uncle, actually ride a few feet before he pitched forward onto the sidewalk. "I did it!" he shouted.

He's going to learn to ride it, thought Ramona, and then I'll get to ride his bicycle.

Willa Jean returned to the accordion as if it might have learned to play while she let it rest, but no, it went right on shrieking and groaning. "I know how I'll make it play," she said.

Ramona turned from the window in time to see Willa Jean set her accordion on one end

17

on the floor. Holding it down with one foot through the strap, she used both hands to stretch it up as high as she could pull it. Then, as Ramona understood what she was about to do and tried to grab her, Willa Jean quickly took her foot out of the strap, turned, sat on the upended accordion, and lifted both feet from the floor. As she sank down, the accordion uttered one long screech, as if it were dying in agony.

"Willa Jean!" cried Ramona, horrified and delighted by the dreadful piercing noise that left her ears ringing. Willa Jean jumped up beaming. The accordion, Ramona could see, would never rise again. Its bellows had split, silencing it forever. "You broke it," Ramona said, knowing she might have done the same thing at Willa Jean's age.

"I don't care," said Willa Jean. "I made a big noise, and now I don't want it anymore."

Mrs. Kemp burst in to see what had happened. "You naughty girls!" she cried when she saw the remains of Uncle Hobart's present.

"But I didn't do it," protested Ramona. "It's not my fault."

"An expensive musical instrument ruined," said Mrs. Kemp. "You're a big girl, Ramona. You should know better than let Willa Jean break it." She turned to her granddaughter. "Aren't you ashamed of yourself?"

"No," said Willa Jean. "It's a dumb old thing that wouldn't play."

"Willa Jean, go to your room," ordered Mrs.

Kemp, who usually felt that anything Willa
Jean did or said was cute, sweet, or adorable.
"I'm ashamed of you, spoiling your nice uncle's
homecoming."

Scowling, Willa Jean did as she was told.

Mrs. Kemp turned to Ramona. "As for you,
young lady, you sit on that chair until your
mother comes for you."

Ramona sat, and Ramona seethed, angry at
the unfairness of all that had happened. Why
should she have to look after Willa Jean when
her mother paid Mrs. Kemp to look after
Ramona? And Uncle Hobart was just plain stupid to give a little girl something she couldn't
use until she was older, but then, grown-ups
were often stupid about presents. Ramona
knew. She had been given books "to grow
into," and by the time she had grown into
them, they had lain around so long they no
longer looked interesting. But an accordion—
growing up to an accordion would take forever.

Outside, other children had come to watch

Howie learn to ride his unicycle. Ramona could hear shouts and laughing, and once in a while, a cheer. It isn't fair, Ramona told herself, even though grown-ups were always telling her life was not fair. It wasn't fair that life wasn't fair.

Ramona watched Mrs. Kemp lovingly polish her new brass tray and coffee pot from Saudi Arabia. *Ping-ping-ping* went the timer on the kitchen stove. Howie burst in crying, one knee of his jeans bloody. Uncle Hobart followed with the unicycle. The afternoon was not fair, but neither was it boring.

"Oh, my goodness," cried Mrs. Kemp. "I knew this would happen. I just knew he would get hurt on that contraption."

Ramona could hear Willa Jean singing from her room:

> *"This old man, he is dumb.*
> *Knick-a-knack paddywhack,*
> *Give a dog a phone,*
> *This old man comes rolling home."*

Ramona smiled. Willa Jean never got the words to songs right.

Ping-ping-ping insisted the timer. "Hobart, turn off the oven and take out the pie while I attend to Howie," directed harassed Mrs. Kemp. Willa Jean stalked into the living room, picked up her camel saddle, and stalked out again. In spite of her bitterness, Ramona found the whole scene most entertaining to watch, better than TV because it was live.

When Howie limped back to the living room with one leg of his jeans rolled up and a bandage on his knee, he sat on the couch feeling sorry for himself. Ramona felt sorry for him, too.

"M-m-m." Uncle Hobart inhaled. "Smell Mom's apple pie. Just what I dreamed of every night when I was overseas." He gave his mother a smacking kiss.

"You're not fooling me." Mrs. Kemp was delighted. "You can't make me believe you dreamed of my apple pie every night. I know you better than that."

Uncle Hobart noticed Ramona imprisoned on a chair. "What's the matter with Howie's girlfriend?" he asked.

Of course, Ramona did not answer a man who did not play fair. He had promised to reform and not tease.

"Hobart, what do you think of a big girl who sits and watches while a little girl breaks her accordion?" Mrs. Kemp, Ramona understood, did not want an answer. She wanted to shame Ramona.

Ramona was suddenly struck by a new and disquieting thought. *Mrs. Kemp did not like her*. Until this minute she had thought all adults were supposed to like all children. She understood by now that misunderstandings were to be expected—she had had several with teachers— and often grown-ups and children did not agree, but things somehow worked out. For a grown-up to actually dislike a child and try to shame her, she was sure had to be wrong, very, very. wrong. She longed for Beezus to come, so she could feel someone was on her side, but Beezus

found more and more excuses to delay coming to
the Kemps' after school.

Uncle Hobart apparently thought he was expected to answer his mother's question. "What
do I think of Ramona? Since she's Howie's
girlfriend, I think she's a great kid. Don't you,
Howie?"

"Oh, shut up, Uncle Hobart." Howie scowled
at the carpet.

Good for you, Howie, thought Ramona. You're on my side.

"Howie!" cried Mrs. Kemp. "That's no way to talk to your uncle."

"I don't care," said Howie. "My knee hurts."

"Really, I don't know what got into you children this afternoon." Mrs. Kemp was thoroughly provoked.

Ramona could have told her in one word: *grown-ups*. Instead, she stared at her book and thought, I am never going to come back here again. Never, never, never. She did not care what anyone said. She did not care what happened. She was not going to be looked after by someone who did not like her.

"Poor Mom," said Uncle Hobart. "How about a piece of your apple pie."

Poor us. Ramona included Howie and Willa Jean in her pity as she wished that someday, just once, she too could sit on an accordion. She knew she never would, even if she had the chance. She had grown past Willa Jean's kind of

25

behavior, which had been fun while it lasted. Ramona smiled as she recalled the happy afternoon she had spent, when she was Willa Jean's age, boring holes in the garage wall with her father's brace and bit—until she was caught.

TWO

Ramona's Problem

At dinner the evening after the accordion incident, the members of the Quimby family were silent and thoughtful, as if they all had serious problems on their minds. They really were thinking about their problems, but they looked thoughtful because they were trying to avoid the bones in the fish they were having for supper. Eating fish with bones without looking thoughtful is impossible. Picky-picky, meowing for his turn, wove himself around their legs.

Ramona, who did not care for fish and was willing to let Picky-picky have her share, wished her mother would say, "Ramona eats like a bird," as if Ramona were unusually delicate and sensitive. Some mothers were like that, but not Mrs. Quimby, who would only say cheerfully, "Eat it anyway," if Ramona complained that she did not like fish.

Since she could not get away with eating like a bird, Ramona poked her fork through her fish to remove every single bone before taking the first bite, and while she pushed, she worried. How was she going to inform her family that she was never going to stay with Mrs. Kemp again? Never, and then what? If she did not stay at the Kemps' after school, her mother might not be able to work in the doctor's office, her father could not go to college, and the whole family would fall over like dominoes pushed by Ramona.

Mr. Quimby laid a fishbone on the edge of his plate. "Has Howie's rich uncle, Old Moneybags, turned up yet?" he said to Ramona. To the cat he said, "Beat it, you furry nuisance."

"Yes," said Ramona, "but he's just a plain man with whiskers and jeans. He doesn't look rich at all."

Mr. Quimby said, "These days, you never can tell by clothes."

"Is he nice?" asked Mrs. Quimby.

"No," said Ramona. "He's the kind of grown-up who teases children and thinks he's funny."

"You know the type," said Beezus. "When I got there, he said, 'Who's this lovely little lady?' And I'm not lovely. I have three pimples, and I look terrible." Beezus worried about her face lately, scrubbing it with medicated soap twice a day and refusing to eat chocolate.

"I'm never going back there after school," Ramona burst out. "I don't care what anybody says. I won't go there again! I'll come home and sit on the steps and freeze, but I will not let that awful Mrs. Kemp look after me again." Tears of anger spilled over her untasted fish.

The family was silent. When no one spoke, Ramona flared again. "Well, I won't, and you can't make me. So there! Mrs. Kemp hates me."

There was a time when Mr. Quimby would have said something such as, "Pull yourself together, Ramona, and eat your dinner." Instead, now that he was studying to be a teacher, he said calmly and quietly, "Tell us about it, Ramona."

This made Ramona feel worse. She did not want her father to be calm and quiet, as if she were sick in bed. She wanted him to be upset and excited, too. Her mother, also quiet, handed her a Kleenex. Ramona mopped her eyes, clutched the Kleenex in a ball, and began. She told about the uncle's presents, the song he sang, Howie's bloody knee, and how Willa Jean broke the accordion. Her parents laughed at that. "That ought to make the neighbors happy," said Mr. Quimby. "Now they're spared the racket."

Ramona managed a shaky laugh, too. Now that she was safely in her own home, she could see the funny side to Uncle Hobart's visit—except her part.

"That must have been an interesting noise," remarked Mrs. Quimby.

"A wonderful noise," agreed Ramona. "A really terrible noise that hurt my ears—Picky-picky, you're tickling—but Mrs. Kemp blamed me for not watching Willa Jean, and that isn't fair. And today I figured out something. Mrs. Kemp doesn't like me. She's never nice and is always blaming me for something I didn't do. I don't care what you do to me. *I am not going back.*"

"Did you ever stop to think, Ramona," said Mrs. Quimby, "that perhaps Mrs. Kemp would rather not be a sitter for you or her grandchildren?"

No, Ramona had not thought of that.

"Women her age were brought up to keep house and take care of children," explained

Mrs. Quimby. "That's all they really know how to do. But now maybe she'd rather be doing something else." She looked thoughtful, not fishbone thoughtful, but really thoughtful.

"She could like me a little bit." Ramona now felt sulky instead of angry.

Beezus spoke up. "Ramona is right. Mrs. Kemp doesn't like either of us. That's why I try to go to Pamela's house after school, or to the library."

"Ramona, what do you think you should do?" asked Mr. Quimby.

Ramona did not want the responsibility of thinking what she should do. She wanted help from a grown-up. Sometimes she thought learning to be a teacher had changed her father. "Why can't I stay home and watch myself?" she asked. "Lots of kids watch themselves when nobody is home."

"And those are the kids who get into trouble—Picky-picky, take your claws out of my leg!—You're my daughter," said Mr. Quimby, "and I don't like the idea of you staying alone."

"Other kids don't watch themselves, they watch TV," said Beezus as she cleared the table.

"I wouldn't watch TV," was Ramona's reckless promise. She whisked her own plate to the kitchen and dumped her fish on Picky-picky's dish. "I would sit on a chair and read a book. Cross my heart and hope to die and stew and fry."

"I wouldn't go that far," said her father, sounding more the way Ramona remembered him before he went back to college.

"I could watch her." Beezus rose from the table to serve canned pears while Ramona followed with a plate of oatmeal cookies. "Lots of girls in junior high baby-sit."

"No dessert for me," whispered Mrs. Quimby.

"I'm not a baby." Ramona wondered why Beezus was willing to give up going to Pamela's house. Pamela had everything—her own TV set, her own telephone. Pamela was popular. All the junior high girls wanted to be like Pamela.

Ramona thought fast. Beezus would act big. Beezus would be bossy. She and Beezus would quarrel with no one to stop them. Beezus might tattle. Sometimes she did, and sometimes she didn't. Of course, Ramona tattled, too, but somehow she felt that was different.

On the other hand, there was Mrs. Kemp. As soon as her son left, she would go back to knitting and disliking Ramona. And there was Howie, her best friend, to think about. On sunny days, and even on damp days, he was off riding his bicycle with the boys in the neighborhood, leaving her stuck with Willa Jean. "Would Beezus get paid?" Ramona demanded.

Silence. "Picky-picky, get *down*," said Mrs. Quimby. The cat, who had gobbled up Ramona's fish, wanted more.

"Well—" said Beezus, "I guess I could sit for nothing. After all, I don't like going to the

Kemps' myself. Mrs. Kemp never makes me feel welcome, and their house always smells of old soup."

"I'm sure Mrs. Kemp would like to be with her son as much as possible while he is here," said Mrs. Quimby. "I could suggest she take a week off. That way, you could try staying home without hurting her feelings, and we could see how it works out."

"She'll be glad to get rid of me." The raw,

hurt feeling inside Ramona was beginning to heal now that her family was trying to help.

"You girls will have to come straight home from school," said Mrs. Quimby, "and promise to behave yourselves. No fighting, and never, never, open the door to strangers."

The sisters promised. "Mother, will you phone Mrs. Kemp now?" Ramona was anxious to have the matter settled before Mrs. Kemp telephoned first to say Ramona was a bad influence on Willa Jean.

Howie's grandmother, as Mrs. Quimby had predicted, was delighted to have more time to spend with her son. "Whee!" cheered Ramona. She was free of Mrs. Kemp for at least a week.

When the meal was over, Beezus went to her room to do her homework. Ramona followed and closed the door behind her. "How come you are willing to stay with me instead of going to Pamela's or Mary Jane's after school?" She could not help feeling suspicious, so unexpected was Beezus's behavior.

"Mary Jane is always practicing the piano, and I'm not speaking to Pamela," said Beezus.

"Why not?" Ramona often yelled at people, but never refused to speak. Nothing could happen if you didn't speak, and she liked things to happen.

Beezus explained. "Pamela is always bragging that *her* father has a *real* job, and she's always asking when *my* father is going to stop fooling around and really go to work. So I don't go to her house anymore, and I don't speak to her."

"Pooh to old Pamela." Ramona chewed a hangnail as painful as her thoughts. "She doesn't have any right to say things like that about Daddy. I won't speak to her either."

"And I heard something Aunt Bea said," continued Beezus. "She said schools are laying off teachers. How do we know Daddy will get a job?"

Ramona, who had imagined every school would want a man as nice as her father, now had a new worry. "You don't think Daddy would go to Gaudy Arabia, do you? Even if it would be warmer than that awful frozen-food warehouse where he works?"

"*Saudi* Arabia," corrected Beezus. "No, I don't. He doesn't know anything about oil except it costs a lot, and do you know what I think?" Beezus did not wait for Ramona to answer. "I think Mother won't be working much longer, because she's going to have a baby."

Ramona sat down on the bed with a thump. A damp, dribbly baby, another Quimby. "Why would Mother do a thing like that when she already has us?"

"Don't ask *me*," said Beezus, "but I'm pretty sure she is."

"Why?" asked Ramona, hoping her sister was wrong.

"Well, you remember how Aunt Bea is always asking Mother how she is feeling, as if she had a special reason for asking?"

Looking back, Ramona realized Beezus was right.

"And Mother doesn't eat dessert anymore,"

continued Beezus, "so she won't gain too much weight."

"Maybe she just doesn't want to get fat." Ramona was doubtful about this. Her mother had always been slender, never worrying about her weight like most mothers.

"And twice, back around Thanksgiving, Mother threw up after breakfast." Beezus added another reason.

"That's nothing," scoffed Ramona. "I've thrown up lots of times, and mince pie always makes me want to urp."

"But ladies who are going to have babies sometimes throw up in the morning," explained Beezus.

"They do?" This was news to Ramona. Beezus might be right. She was interested in such things. "Why don't we go ask Mother?"

"When she wants us to know, she will tell us. And of course, I might be wrong. . . ." Doubt crept into Beezus's voice before she said, "Oh, I hope I'm right. I love babies. I'd love to help take care of one of our own. I just know it would be darling."

Ramona sat on the bed thinking while Beezus opened her books. A little brother or sister? She did not like the idea, not one bit. If she had a little brother or sister, grown-ups would say in their knowing way, as if children could not understand, Somebody's nose is out of joint. Ramona had heard them say it many times about children who had new babies in the family. This was their way of talking about children behind their backs in front of them.

"But if it's true, I sure hope Daddy finds a teaching job fast," said Beezus. "Now go away. I have to study."

Ramona wandered into the living room, where her mother was lying on the couch watching the evening news on TV with the sound turned low so it would not disturb her husband, who was studying at the dining room table. Ramona knew she was not supposed to interrupt when he was studying, but this time

41

she decided he wasn't really working, just doodling on a piece of scratch paper with a worried look on his face. She slipped her head up between his ribs and arm.

"Hi," said her father, as if Ramona had brought his thoughts back to the dining room.

"Hi," answered Ramona as her father quickly turned over his page of doodles, but not before she had a glimpse of dollar signs and babies, doodles that must mean he was thinking about a baby.

"You have me to be your little girl," Ramona reminded her father.

Her father rubbed his chin against the top of Ramona's head. "That's right, and I'm mighty glad I do."

"Then you wouldn't want another little girl, would you?" Ramona had to find out.

"Oh, I don't know," said Mr. Quimby. "I like little girls."

THREE

Being Good

On Monday, Howie looked troubled when Ramona hopped off the school bus and turned toward her house instead of his. "Well—so long, Ramona," he said. "See you tomorrow."

"Have fun with your uncle," said Ramona, and walked down Klickitat Street to the Quimby house, where she found the hidden key, let herself in the back door, washed her hands, ate an apple, put the core in the garbage, changed from school clothes into old jeans and a T-shirt, and sat down on the couch to read. She felt grown-up and very, very good. How peaceful the Quimby house was compared to the Kemp house, where the television set was always tuned to soap operas and Willa Jean hopped around, yelling and insisting that Ramona play with her. Being good wasn't going to be hard after all.

Beezus came home a short time later. The sisters greeted one another with unusual courtesy, so determined were they to be good. Beezus took an apple into her room, where she settled down to do her homework.

Picky-picky meowed to be let out of the basement.

"Ramona, will you please let the cat out?" Ordinarily, Beezus would have shouted, Can't you hear Picky-picky? Let him out.

Another time, Ramona would have shouted back, Let him out yourself. He's more your cat than mine. I wasn't even born when we got him. Today she answered, "Yes, Beezus," as she opened the basement door.

Picky-picky immediately went to his dish to see if someone had surprised him with a choice tidbit. Ramona returned to her book. Picky-picky, finding only leftover Puss-puddy, strolled out of the kitchen and went to the couch, where he waggled his rear end as if he were about to jump up beside Ramona. The effort was too great for his old age. Ramona, who was always pleased to receive attention from the cat, lifted him gently. He curled up beside her and purred as if his purring machinery had grown rusty and was wearing out.

Of course, the girls' parents, when they came home, were delighted to see what well-behaved daughters they had. The girls looked closely at their mother's waistline to see if she had gained weight since breakfast.

Tuesday afternoon was much the same as Monday. Beezus talked a long time on the telephone to a friend Ramona did not know. The conversation was about who said what to a new boy at school, and what was printed on someone's T-shirt, and how some girl said she had seen some boy looking at Beezus, because Beezus said, "Do you think he looked at me, *really*?" and on and on. When the conversation, uninteresting to Ramona, finally ended, Beezus went into the bathroom and scrubbed her face with medicated soap.

"What good girls we have," said Mrs. Quimby when she returned from work with her waistline no larger than it had been the day before. However, she did look tired, and on the way home, had bought a pizza for dinner. Since pizzas were an extravagance in the Quimby household, this meant she did not feel like cooking dinner.

By Wednesday Ramona began to dread being good because being good was boring, so she was happy to see Howie coming down the street, wheeling his bicycle with his unicycle balanced across the seat and handlebars. She was even happier when he laid both on her driveway. Ramona met him at the door.

"Come on out, Ramona," said Howie. "Uncle Hobart helped me learn to ride my unicycle, so now you can ride my bicycle."

Ramona's wish had come true. "Hey, Beezus," she shouted, "I'm going out and ride Howie's bike."

"You're supposed to ask first," said Beezus. "You can't go out unless I say so."

Ramona felt that Beezus was showing off in

front of Howie. "How come you're so bossy all of a sudden?" she demanded.

"Mom and Dad left me in charge, and you have to mind," answered Beezus.

"You talk the way you and Mary Jane used to talk when you played house and made me be the baby. Well, I'm not a baby now." Ramona grew more determined and contrary. "Mom always lets me go out and play with Howie."

"Just the same, if you get hurt, I'm responsible," said Beezus.

"You're just being mean," said Ramona. "So long, Pizzaface." Just before she slammed the

door, she was horrified to see Beezus's face crumple, as if she were about to burst into tears.

Howie cried out, "Ramona, look at me!"

Ramona watched Howie mount his unicycle and ride it to the corner and back, but as she watched, she felt puzzled and uncomfortable. She had made Beezus unhappy, but why? She did not understand. She had called Beezus Pieface many times without upsetting her. What was so different about Pizzaface? She happened to think of it because they had eaten pizza the night before, and pizza was a sort of pie.

"Good work, Howie," said Ramona when he had ridden to the corner and back a second time. But what about me? She thought, still worrying about Beezus. I can't spend the rest of my life sitting on a couch being good.

"Come on, ride my bike," said Howie. "Let's see if we can make it around the block."

Ramona raised Howie's bicycle, made sure

one pedal was high and the other low so she would have a good start, mounted, and rode wobbling down the sidewalk.

"Atta girl, Ramona," said Howie, seating himself on his unicycle and pedaling ahead of her.

Ramona wobbled along after him, and as she wobbled, she worried. What was Beezus going to say to their mother and father? Would she have to go back to the Kemps'?

By the time Ramona reached the corner, she was less wobbly. She even managed to turn the corner without tipping over. She began to pedal faster. Now she was really riding, filled with joy, as if she were flying.

Ramona passed Howie. She stood up on the pedals to go faster. Ramona's mind was on speed, not balance, and at the next corner, as she turned, she lost control. Down she went, with the bicycle on top of her. Her left knee and elbow hurt; her breath was knocked out of her.

Howie dropped his unicycle and came running to lift his bicycle from Ramona. "You okay?" he asked.

Ramona rose stiffly to her feet. "I don't think anything's broken," she said, struggling not to cry. Blood was running down her scraped elbow and soaking the knee of her jeans. Limping, she wheeled the bicycle, and Howie wheeled his unicycle, as far as her driveway.

"Come back again, Howie," said Ramona. "I love to ride your bicycle, even if I did take a spill."

"Sure, Ramona," agreed Howie. "You better go mop up all that blood."

When Ramona went to the back door so she wouldn't bleed on the living room carpet, she had to knock because the door was locked. When Beezus opened it, she ignored her sister's dripping blood and returned to her room without speaking.

Ramona limped to the bathroom. Maybe she could make Beezus speak if she let her know

53

she had been right, that Ramona had hurt herself when she disobeyed. She said in her most pitiful voice, "Beezus, I had a bad fall. Come and help me."

"I don't care, you hateful little creep," was her sister's answer. "Serves you right. I'm not speaking to you anymore. It's not my fault my face is all red and blotchy like a pizza."

What Ramona heard left her speechless, ashamed, and angry. She had hurt her sister's feelings accidentally; Beezus had hurt hers on purpose, and she didn't even care that Ramona was dripping blood. She was probably *glad*. Bossy old Beezus.

Ramona washed her own knee and elbow, sprayed them with disinfectant, plastered them with Band-Aids, and changed into clean jeans and a long-sleeved blouse to hide her wounds. She then lifted Picky-picky to the couch, sat down beside him to read and be good Ramona again.

Ramona, however, found she could not read,

she felt so terrible, even though she was angry, about hurting her sister's feelings in a way she had not intended. The girls often called one another names—Beezus called Ramona Dribblepuss when her ice cream melted from a cone and trickled down her chin—but they never used really unkind names. Now Beezus called her a hateful little creep and meant it. And what if Beezus told their mother and father they had quarreled? Then it would be back to the Kemps' for Ramona.

Good girl that she was, Ramona decided to set the table. She heard Beezus go into the bathroom and wash her face before coming into the kitchen. Picky-picky managed to get down from the couch and follow her, in case she decided to feed him. Beezus scrubbed four potatoes and put them in the oven to bake. Then she picked up the cat, hugged and petted him. "Nice Picky-picky," she said so Ramona could hear. This, of course, meant that Ramona was not nice.

However, when their parents came home, Beezus acted as if nothing had happened, and so did Ramona—except they both talked to their mother and father but not to one another. Ramona thought maybe the white uniform her mother wore to work in the doctor's office looked tighter at the waist. Perhaps it had shrunk, or last night's pizza had been fattening, or maybe Beezus was right—she was going to have a baby.

As the family was about to sit down to dinner, the telephone rang, and since Mrs. Quimby happened to be standing near it, she answered. "Oh, I'm fine," she said.

Ramona wanted to look at Beezus. However, they were not only not speaking, they were not looking. She listened intently to their mother's side of the telephone conversation.

Mrs. Quimby was smiling. "Yes . . . yes, of course. I think that's a great idea . . . no, it doesn't hurt to try, so go ahead . . . it sounds like fun. Let me know how it turns out."

"What sounds like fun?" demanded Ramona and Beezus at the same time.

"Oh—something," said Mrs. Quimby airily, and winked at her husband. "I can't remember exactly what."

"You winked at Daddy," Ramona accused her mother, as if winking were somehow wicked.

"Mom! You're fibbing!" cried Beezus in exasperation. "You can too remember."

"It isn't nice to talk about things in front of people and not tell them what you are talking about." Ramona suffered from curiosity as much as Beezus.

"Who called?" asked Mr. Quimby.

Ha! thought Ramona, now we've got her. She won't fib to Dad.

"Howie's mother," said Mrs. Quimby. "She needed some information."

"Oh," was all the girls' father had to say.

"Is it about a birthday party?" asked Ramona, because her mother had mentioned fun.

"Never mind, Ramona," said her mother. "Just eat your dinner."

"Well, is it?" persisted Ramona.

"No, it isn't a birthday party," said Mrs. Quimby, "and it doesn't concern you."

Ramona hoped her mother was still fibbing. She wanted fun to concern herself.

The parents did not notice that the girls were not speaking—or if they did, they chose not to mention the matter.

After dinner, Mrs. Quimby said she was a little tired and thought she would go to bed and read awhile. The girls avoided looking at one another, even though the remark was significant.

"I'll do the dishes," volunteered Mr. Quimby as the girls cleared the table. "Then I'll work on my lesson plan for tomorrow's practice teaching." He lowered his voice. "And I want to make one thing clear to you girls. You are not to do anything to worry your mother. Do you understand?"

The girls nodded, avoiding one another's eyes. From the exasperation in their father's voice, they knew he understood they had quarreled. Beezus went off to her room.

Ramona yearned to follow her sister, to say she was sorry, that she had not meant Pizzaface the way Beezus thought she meant it, to find out what Beezus thought of the mysterious telephone call, to ask when she thought her mother was going to have a baby—if she was.

However, Ramona was not used to saying she was sorry, especially to someone who was bossy and called her a hateful little creep. Little creep she could overlook, but not hateful little creep.

FOUR

Picky-picky

Strangely, when Ramona's heart was heavy, so were her feet. She trudged to the school bus, plodded through the halls at school, and clumped home from the bus after school. The house felt lonely when she let herself in, so she turned on the television set for company. She sat on the couch and stared at one of the senseless soap operas Mrs. Kemp watched. They were all about rich people—none of them looking like Howie's Uncle Hobart—who accused

61

other people of doing something terrible; Ramona didn't understand exactly what, but it all was boring, boring, boring.

Beezus came home, left her books in her room, and probably hung up her jacket instead of throwing it on her bed. She then went to the basement door, her back saying silently to Ramona, *You* didn't let Picky-picky out. Ramona realized she had not let the cat out because she had not heard him meow.

When Beezus opened the door, no cat came out to investigate his dish. Beezus snapped on the basement light and descended the steps.

That's funny, thought Ramona.

"Ramona!" screamed Beezus. "Come quick!"

At last! Beezus had spoken, but her voice told Ramona something dreadful must have happened. Frightened, Ramona ran down the basement steps, skipping the last two and jumping to the concrete floor. Her sister needed her.

Beezus, with her hands clasped to her chest, was standing over Picky-picky's basket. "He's *dead*." Beezus stared at the motionless cat in disbelief, tears in her eyes. "Picky-picky is *dead*."

"How can he be?" asked Ramona. "He was alive this morning." Both girls had forgotten, or at least put aside, their feelings toward one another.

"He just is," said Beezus. "I don't know why, unless he died of old age. I started to pick him up, and he's all limp and cold. Go ahead and touch him and you'll see."

Ramona summoned courage to touch timidly with one finger the lifeless Picky-picky. He felt like cold, limp fur.

"What are we going to do?" asked distraught Beezus.

"Wait till Mother and Daddy come home," suggested Ramona.

"But Daddy said we weren't to worry Mother," Beezus reminded her. The sisters looked helplessly at one another. "I know we didn't do anything to Picky-picky, but I think coming home and finding a dead cat in the basement would upset her a lot."

"Yes," agreed Ramona. "It sure would, especially at dinner time." The two looked sadly at the remains of their pet. "I guess we should bury him," said Ramona, "and have a funeral."

"We'll have to hurry," said Beezus, "and I

don't know if I can dig a grave." She lifted her father's heavy shovel from the wall, where it hung upside down between two nails, and started up the steps. "Come on, help me find a place."

Ramona was glad to follow. Somehow she did not want to be alone with the ghost of Picky-picky. Silly, but that was the way she felt.

The girls walked across the wet grass to choose a spot in the corner of the backyard where their father had grubbed out an old laurel bush that had grown too large for the space. Beezus jabbed the shovel into the muddy soil, stepped on the top of the blade to push it farther down, lifted out a shovelful of dirt, and laid it aside. "What will we bury him in?" she asked, struggling with another shovelful of wet dirt.

"I'll find a box." Now that Beezus was speaking to her, Ramona was eager to do her part. Besides, even though she felt sad and awed by her first experience with the death of someone she knew—birds didn't count—burying the cat was interesting. In the basement she picked up a cardboard carton and ran upstairs. In her room she found a doll's pillow and two doll's blankets. She lined the box with one blanket and placed the pillow at one end. She forced herself to return to the basement, where she found she could not bring herself to lift the lifeless Picky-picky. She would leave that to Beezus.

Out in the backyard, Ramona found Beezus panting as she wrestled with the shovel. "Let me try," she offered, but soon discovered the shovel was too long and unwieldy for her to manage. "I'll get a trowel," she said. Together, the girls worked, Ramona on her knees digging with the trowel and finally with her hands, until they had dug a small grave just right for a cat. "Beezus, will you put Picky-picky in the box?" asked Ramona. "I'm—not exactly scared, but I don't want to."

Back in the basement, Beezus lifted Picky-picky into his cardboard coffin and laid his head on the pillow. Ramona tucked the second doll blanket around him, and together they set the lid in place.

Beezus carried the box out to the gravesite. "It doesn't seem right just to bury him," she said, "and I don't remember much about Grandma Day's funeral except everyone whispered, there were lots of flowers, and I had to sit very still. You were just a baby then."

Ramona knew about funerals. "On TV when they bury somebody, they stand around the grave and pray," she said. "Then the wife of the dead person cries until someone leads her away."

"I suppose we should pray." Beezus sounded uncertain as to the proper way to pray for a cat.

Ramona had no doubts. She bowed her head and began, "Now I lay me down to sleep—"

"That's not right," interrupted Beezus. "You're not the one who's being buried."

"Oh. Okay." Ramona began again. "Now we lay Picky-picky down to sleep. We pray thee, Lord, his soul to keep. Thy love stay with him through the night and wake him with the morning light. Amen." When she finished the prayer, she said, "There. That's that."

Beezus frowned in thought. "But he won't wake with the morning light. He isn't supposed to. He's dead."

Ramona was not worried. "Cats have nine lives, so tomorrow he will wake up someplace as somebody's kitten and start a new life."

"I hadn't thought of that," said Beezus, "but it sounds logical. I hope his new owners give him melon rind. Picky-picky loved melon rind." She picked up the shovel and began to fill in the grave. "We should have some flowers for him, but there aren't any."

"I wonder which of his lives we got him on," said Ramona as she gathered damp brown leaves to strew on the grave. The girls stood looking sadly at the little mound left by Picky-picky's coffin. "He was a good cat," said Ramona, "even if he didn't like me much when I was little."

"I can barely remember when he was a little tiny kitten who climbed the curtains," said Beezus.

"I'll make him a tombstone." After sharing the sad experience, Ramona felt closer to her sister, close enough to speak of something other than their cat.

"Beezus—" she said with a gulp. "I'm sorry about yesterday when I called you—you know—and I didn't mean it the way you took it." She explained how she happened to change Pieface to Pizzaface. "I didn't mean to hurt your feelings. I—I won't say it again, no matter how mad I get."

"That's okay," said Beezus with a big sigh. "I shouldn't have been so cross with you. Mom says I'll outgrow skin problems, but it seems like forever. Now maybe I better put something on these blisters on my hands."

In spite of the funeral, Ramona felt light and happy. She and her sister had both apologized and forgiven one another. "And we didn't worry Mother," Ramona pointed out as she skipped off to the basement to find a short board in a pile of scrap lumber.

By the time Beezus had changed out of her muddy clothes, scrubbed her hands, applied disinfectant, and covered her blisters with Band-Aids, the grave bore a marker made from a scrap of board. Printed in crayon were the words:

Picky-Picky
Quimby
Age 10 years
A good cat

Beneath the words, Ramona had drawn a picture of a yellow cat.

"But we'll have to tell Mother and Daddy," said Beezus. "They're sure to miss him."

"Won't that upset Mother?" asked Ramona.

Beezus was filled with uncertainty. "Well—I don't think our burying him will upset her as much as finding him dead in the basement." She rearranged the Band-Aids on her hands. "You'd better get into some clean clothes, or she'll really be upset. And don't forget to use the nailbrush on your fingernails."

Before the girls had time to change their clothes, their parents came home. As Mr. Quimby set a bag of groceries on the kitchen counter, he looked at his younger daughter and remarked with a grin, "Add water and get instant Ramona. You'd better add some soap, too."

Mrs. Quimby, used to seeing Ramona covered with dirt, only said, "I found a bargain in cat food."

Ramona exchanged an anguished look with her sister and went off to scrub her hands and change to clean clothes. What a waste of money, buying cat food now. The sisters exchanged another anguished look when Ramona returned to set the table. Beezus was washing lettuce with the tips of her fingers to keep her Band-Aid dry.

"Why Beezus, what has happened to your hands?" asked her mother as she laid a bunch of carrots on the counter. "You've hurt yourself."

"It's nothing much," said Beezus.

"Here, let me finish the lettuce," said Mr. Quimby as he took one of his daughter's hands to examine her wounds. "Why, this is terrible," he said. "How did you get all those blisters?"

Beezus did not want to tell. She cast a look at Ramona that asked, What do I do now?

This is dumb, thought Ramona. Their parents had to know sometime. "She blistered her hands digging a hole in the backyard," she informed her parents and added in her saddest, most sorrowful voice, "a little grave. We dug a little grave." She really enjoyed the looks of astonishment the announcement produced.

Mr. Quimby, who was first to recover, looked amused. "And whom, may I ask, or what did you bury in a grave big enough to raise blisters on Beezus's hands?"

Ramona knew he was thinking of the little graves they had dug for dead birds when they were younger. She sighed to make her announcement seem even more mournful. "We buried Picky-picky. He passed away today."

The parents' look of surprise and amusement turned to shock. They looked even more shocked than Ramona had expected. She began to feel frightened. Perhaps she had upset her mother after all.

"Why, you poor children—" said Mrs. Quimby with tears in her eyes. "Burying the cat all by yourselves."

"Why didn't you wait for me?" asked their father. "I could have taken care of him."

"You said we shouldn't upset Mother," explained Beezus. "And we didn't want her to come home and find Picky-picky dead."

"We made a nice grave, with leaves and a marker," said Ramona. "And we remembered to say a prayer like they do on TV before somebody leads the dead person's wife away."

Mrs. Quimby brushed away a tear with the back of her hand. "I'm a very lucky mother to have such dear girls," she said.

"And I'm really proud of you," said Mr. Quimby. "I hope we have such good luck the next time."

The sisters stared at their mother's waistline. Her uniform was tight. It was not their imagination. They raised their eyes to her face. She was smiling.

"Then it's true!" Beezus was filled with excitement and joy.

"You're going to have a baby." Although she had suspected the truth, Ramona was as disbelieving as if she were charging her mother with magic.

74

"When are you going to have it?" asked Beezus.

"In July," confessed her mother.

"Correction," said Mr. Quimby. "*We* are going to have a baby. I'm going to be a proud father."

"You just said you were proud of *us*," Ramona reminded him.

"So I did," said her father. "But now I can be proud of three instead of two."

"And I don't think we need worry about leaving the girls alone until I stop working," said Mrs. Quimby.

"Whee!" cried Ramona. "No more Mrs. Kemp!" At the same time she was thinking, a third Quimby child? Her mind was full of excited questions, but deep down inside where she hid her most secret thoughts, Ramona realized she would lose her favored place as the baby of the family. She would become the middle child, neither big nor little. She thought maybe she would rather have another cat.

FIVE

"IT"

Now that the news of the baby was out, Beezus and Ramona had no more trouble getting along with one another after school. Saying they were sorry and burying Picky-picky had brought them closer together. Their parents said nothing more about their returning to the Kemps' after school.

Ramona began to feel that life was humdrum. Even the weather was dreary—wet and cold, but not cold enough to snow. She tried

76

wearing a Chiquita banana sticker plastered to her forehead when she went to school, to start a fad like the sticker fad in Aunt Beatrice's third grade. Her aunt said she sometimes felt as if she were teaching a bunch of bananas. Members of Ramona's class said, "What are you wearing that for?" or "That looks dumb."

Then Ramona tried announcing, "We're going to have a new baby at our house." No one was interested. New babies were common in the families of her classmates. Because she

had been to their homes, Ramona knew what new babies meant—a stroller in the hall, a playpen in the living room, a high chair in the kitchen, tiny clothes strewn around, plastic toys underfoot, zwieback crumbs sticking to chairs. Of course she could not expect her friends to get excited about the Quimbys' new baby.

Weeks went by. Aunt Beatrice telephoned almost every evening to ask how her sister was feeling. The conversation of the grown-up sisters was filled with laughter, which puzzled Ramona and Beezus, who failed to see why having a baby was funny. They hung around, trying to guess what the laughter was about from their mother's side of the mysterious conversations. They were able to guess that Aunt Bea was very busy, that she went skiing almost every weekend, but the ski season would soon be over. Their mother's remarks were meaningless. "Why, Bea!" "I don't believe it!" "What did Michael say?" "No. No, I won't tell the girls."

Both Beezus and Ramona pounced on their mother when a conversation ended. "What won't you tell us?" they demanded.

"If I told you, you would know," answered their mother.

"Mother-*er*!" protested Ramona. "You're just plain mean."

"Yes, exasperating," agreed Beezus.

"Me?" Mrs. Quimby looked innocent. "Mean? Exasperating? Wherever did you get that idea?"

"Did Michael ask Aunt Bea to marry him?" demanded Beezus, eager for romance.

"Not that I know of," answered their provoking mother.

Ramona stamped her foot. "Mother, you stop it! You're getting to be as bad as Howie's Uncle Hobart, always teasing."

"Heaven forbid that I should be like Howie's Uncle Hobart," answered Mrs. Quimby, still teasing. "I'll have to try to mend my ways."

Ramona was strict with her mother. "See

that you do," she said. "I don't like mysteries, except in books."

Mr. Quimby, who was trying to study at the dining room table, frowned during all these conversations that disturbed his work. Something dreadful called a midterm was about to happen at the university. He was worried and nervous. The girls could tell because he made more jokes than usual. When he was worried, he always joked. When he saw Ramona lying on the floor looking at TV, he said, "There's Ramona. Batteries not included."

However, Mr. Quimby's studies would be over the middle of June, when he would receive his teaching credential a few weeks before the baby, known as It, was due. Then he would work during the summer as a checker at one of the Shop-rite markets to replace checkers who took vacations. By September, he would have found a place in a school, if not in Portland, at least in a suburb. Mrs. Quimby would leave her job to take care of It, which pleased

Ramona. The house always seemed so empty without her mother.

Of course, Beezus and Ramona were eager to know if It would be a boy or girl. Ramona wanted a boy. Beezus wanted a girl. Their parents said they would take whatever came along.

The girls were concerned with other questions. Whose room would It share? How long would their mother stay home to take care of It? Ramona wanted her mother home for keeps—babies weren't much work, they just lay around all day. Maybe her mother could find time to let down the hems of Ramona's skirts and pants and bake a few cookies. Beezus wished she could stay home from school to take care of It herself. However, she had the summer to look forward to. Mrs. Quimby said that after the girls' father found a job and It was a few months old, she would like to take some evening courses at the University. "And I'll take care of It while you study," said Beezus.

"Enough of It," said Mr. Quimby. "No child

of ours is going to be called It Quimby. Think how everyone would laugh when the teacher called the roll. How would you feel introducing your new brother or sister by saying, 'This is It'? And every time anyone said, 'I don't like it,' about bread pudding or stupid TV programs, It's feelings would be hurt."

The family agreed that of course the baby needed a real name. Robert Quimby, Junior? Maybe, if It turned out to be a boy. Mrs. Quimby said the baby would not be named after herself because she had never liked being called Dorothy. Ramona thought Aston Martin would be good for a boy. She had heard the name someplace and thought it sounded nice. Beezus preferred Gary or Burt for a boy and thought April was a pretty name for a girl, except It would be born in July, which was not a name for a person.

Then Mr. Quimby brought home a pamphlet from the drugstore, called *A Name for Your Baby*, which listed names and their meanings.

Ramona immediately found her own name and discovered that Ramona meant "wise helper." How boring, she thought, and hoped this did not mean that she would be expected to change It's diapers or anything like that.

Beezus, on the other hand, laughed when she discovered Beatrice meant "heavenly one." "Whee!" she said, twirling around the living room and flapping her arms like wings. Her complexion had improved, which made her happier about everything.

Together the girls studied the pamphlet. Many names would not do at all. Philbert, which meant "superior," sounded good with Quimby, but at school, boys would call him a nut. Beezus thought Abelard might be a good name for a boy because it meant "romantic hero," but Ramona pointed out that everyone at school would call him "Lard." Beezus also thought Lorelei, which meant "romantic siren," was a pretty name for a girl until Ramona began to chant, "Loreliar, Loreliar, pants on fire."

Ramona preferred Gwendolyn for a girl because the name meant "fair." If she had to have another sister, she wanted one who always played fair.

Mr. Quimby suggested names that were much too fancy—Alphonso Horatio, Clarinda Hepzibah, or Quentin Quincy Quimby. His daughters, however, did not take him seriously. This was more of his joking because he was worried.

"What if It is twins?" Ramona's thought presented a whole new problem. She studied the pamphlet once more. Paul and Pauline? Boris and Doris? Gerald and Geraldine?

"They could be two girls or two boys," Beezus pointed out.

"Abby and Gabby," said Mr. Quimby. "Peter and Mosquiter."

"Daddy, you're just being silly." Ramona was always stern with her father when she felt he had gone too far with his jokes.

Mrs. Quimby asked what was wrong with

plain names like Jane or John. Nothing, agreed her daughters, but fancy names were more fun to look up. They discovered that Hobart meant "clever," but of course they weren't going to name their baby after Howie's uncle.

Finally It came to be known as Algie. When Mrs. Quimby could no longer squeeze into her clothes and changed to maternity clothes, Mr. Quimby recited:

"Algie went out walking.
Algie met a bear.
The bear was bulgy.
The bulge was Algie."

Mrs. Quimby said, "You wouldn't think it was so funny if men had babies." However, she laughed and referred to the new baby as Algie after that. The girls, when told that Algie was short for Algernon, looked up the name and discovered it meant "courageous."

"Of course, we couldn't really name it Algernon," said practical Beezus. "Everyone at school would make fun of him. Nobody is named Algernon except in old-fashioned books."

Besides the fun of finding names, Beezus and Mrs. Quimby watched for sales of baby clothes. Ramona's diapers, inherited from Beezus, had long ago been used for dust cloths, much to Ramona's relief. She did not like to be reminded that she had ever worn diapers. "On TV, babies wear disposable diapers," she told her mother.

"Much too expensive," said Mrs. Quimby.

All the Quimbys' needs seemed too expensive. Still no letters arrived asking Mr. Quimby to report for an interview. "Maybe I should go to Saudi Arabia like Old Moneybags, work double shifts, and earn enough to pay off our bills and the mortgage, and buy a car that wouldn't eat us out of house and home in repair bills," he said thoughtfully. This time his daughters were sure he was joking.

"Bob, please be practical," said Mrs. Quimby.

"You have no engineering experience." Because she needed exercise, she left for her evening walk.

Ramona decided to go along because she wanted to talk privately to her mother. As they walked beneath the budding trees, she began by saying, "When Algie comes, I won't be your baby anymore."

"That's right," agreed her mother. "You will be my middle child, with a special place right in the middle of my heart. And when Algie comes, I will be home, so we can spend more time together. Daddy will have found a teaching job by then."

Ramona was comforted. They walked in silence for a while before she asked another question that had been worrying her. "Does Algie hurt you?"

Mrs. Quimby's smile was reassuring. "No, he doesn't hurt me, but he does kick." She laid Ramona's hand on the bulge that was Algie, and sure enough, Ramona felt a kick so tiny it was almost a flutter. Ramona was stunned by

the miracle of that little kick and was silent all the way home.

Mr. Quimby began to work double shifts weekends at the frozen-food warehouse. He looked so tired and discouraged that his daughters were frightened. Somewhere, someplace, there must be a school that wanted their father. Nothing in the world was worse than unhappy parents. Nothing. When parents were unhappy, the whole world seemed to go wrong. The weather even seemed rainier, although this was probably in Beezus's and Ramona's imaginations. Their part of Oregon was noted for rain.

Then one day a letter did arrive, offering Mr. Quimby a teaching position in a one-room schoolhouse, grades one through eight, in a town no one had ever heard of, in southeastern Oregon. Beezus ran out to the car for the road map. "That's *miles* away," she said when she had searched the map and found the town. "It's miles from anyplace. It isn't even on a red line on the map. It's on a black and white line, almost in Idaho."

"What's in that part of the country?" wondered Mrs. Quimby who, along with her husband, had lived in Oregon all her life but never visited that corner of the state.

"Sagebrush, I guess." Mr. Quimby was vague. "Juniper, lava rocks. I don't know."

"Sheep. I learned that in school." Beezus did not seem happy about her knowledge.

"Hooray for the Portland public schools." Mr. Quimby's hooray did not express excitement.

"Lambs are cute," ventured Ramona, hoping to make her father feel better about his offer.

"But our house," said Mrs. Quimby, "and a new baby." No one had thought that the family might have to move.

"And Picky-picky's grave." Ramona assumed her most sorrowful expression. "We would have to leave his little grave."

"If I were single," Mr. Quimby seemed to be

thinking out loud, "I might enjoy teaching in a one-room schoolhouse for a year or two."

But you've got us, thought Ramona, and I don't want to leave Howie and my friends at school and Aunt Bea and all our nice neighbors.

"It sounds like Laura Ingalls Wilder," said Beezus, "only with sheep."

"Bob—" Mrs. Quimby hesitated. "If you want to take the job, we could rent our house. A small town might be an interesting experience for the girls until you found a job in the city."

Strangers in their house, some bratty child in her room, marking up her walls with crayons. Please, Daddy, thought Ramona with clenched fists, please, please say no.

Mr. Quimby sat tapping the end of a ball-point pen against his teeth. His family waited, each thinking of the changes that might be made in her life. "No freeways," he said, as if he were still thinking out loud. "Blue skies, wide open spaces."

"We have blue skies here," said Ramona. "Except when it rains."

"No big library," said Beezus. "Maybe no library at all."

Mrs. Quimby kissed her husband on the forehead. "Why don't we think it over a few days? Now that you've had one offer, another might come along."

"Good idea," announced Mr. Quimby, "but I need a steady income, and soon." He patted the bulge that was Algie.

"Daddy," ventured Ramona, "if you don't teach in that school, promise you won't leave us and go to that Arabian Nights place. Please."

"Not with Algie on the way." Mr. Quimby hugged Ramona. "Anyway, I understand that camels spit."

"Just like Howie's Uncle Hobart used to do," said Ramona.

Somehow the whole family felt better knowing that one school wanted Mr. Quimby, even if he was not sure he wanted the school.

SIX

A Surprise, Sort Of

Howie, who was beginning to wish his Uncle Hobart would go back to Saudi Arabia so he could sleep in his own room again, brought his bicycle and unicycle over to the Quimbys' every day after school. Beezus never again objected to Ramona's riding around the block.

Ramona thought how lonely she would be without Howie if she had to go live in the land of sheep. "Maybe we will move away to southeastern Oregon," she confided.

94

"Hey, that would be neat," said Howie. "They have wild horses down there. Maybe you could send me one."

Ramona was offended. Howie wouldn't even miss her. "I wouldn't send you one even if I could catch it," she informed him.

Howie understood. "I didn't mean I wouldn't miss you," he said. "I only meant if you have to leave and if catching a horse would be easy."

Since no more offers of teaching positions arrived, no matter how often the family looked in the mailbox, Ramona saw that moving from Klickitat Street was a very real possibility.

One afternoon before Howie arrived, the telephone rang. Ramona beat Beezus to answering it.

"Ramona?" It was Willa Jean.

"Willa Jean!" Ramona was astonished. "I didn't know you knew how to dial."

"Uncle Hobart showed me," explained Willa Jean. "Ramona, come back and play with me. Please. It's lonesome here with Grandma."

Ramona felt sad and guilty. "I'm sorry, Willa Jean, I can't. Maybe your Uncle Hobart will play with you."

"He's not around much," said Willa Jean. "He has a girlfriend, and anyway, he's a grown-up."

"I know," said Ramona, meaning she knew he was a grown-up, not that he had a girl-friend."

"Good-bye." Willa Jean, who had nothing more to say, hung up.

Ramona sighed. She remembered what it was like to be the littlest child in the neighbor-hood. She remembered all too well the days back in kindergarten when she was known as Ramona the Pest. Maybe she could ask Howie to bring Willa Jean over to play sometime when her mother stopped working. Nursery school had done Willa Jean a world of good, as all the grown-ups except Mrs. Kemp said. Mrs. Kemp thought Willa Jean was perfect to begin with.

On the bus the next morning, Ramona sat

beside Howie. "Willa Jean says your Uncle Hobart has a girlfriend."

"Yeah." Howie wasn't much interested. "Some teacher."

A terrible suspicion crossed Ramona's mind. "What teacher?" she asked.

"I don't know," said Howie. "He acts like it's a big secret. Maybe she has two heads or something."

Ramona was silent all the way to school. She had that sinking feeling she always felt when she rode down in an elevator. She knew—she just *knew*—that Howie's uncle was seeing her aunt. She didn't know why she knew, but she knew.

After school, Ramona confided her fears to her sister, who said, "Oh, I don't think that could be—Aunt Beatrice and Uncle Hobart." She spoke so doubtfully that Ramona knew Beezus thought she might be right.

"Maybe that's what the big secret is. Mom doesn't want us to know because we don't like

97

Uncle Hobart. She thinks we might say something to Aunt Beatrice."

"Oh well," said Ramona, "he'll have to go back to Saudi Arabia sometime. Then we'll be rid of him."

"I wonder what happened to Michael," Beezus thought aloud.

Then one Sunday Mrs. Quimby told the girls to set two extra places at the table for dinner.

"Who's coming?" asked Ramona.

"Your Aunt Bea and a friend." Mrs. Quimby was smiling.

"What friend?" demanded both girls.

"Oh, just a friend," answered their maddening mother.

"A man?" asked Beezus.

"Girls, I really don't have time to play guessing games." Mrs. Quimby turned her attention to something on the stove.

"It's a man." Ramona was positive. "It's Howie's uncle."

Mrs. Quimby looked startled. "How did you know?"

"Oh, a little bird told me." Ramona tried to sound as annoying as any grown-up.

Beezus was indignant. "You mean Aunt Bea is bringing that awful man *here*? How did she meet him?"

"He remembered her from high school and asked Howie's mother about her. She called to ask if I thought my sister remembered him, and I said she did, so he phoned her, and now they're coming to dinner."

So that was what the mysterious telephone calls were all about, thought Ramona, but she said, "Well, he better not spit around here."

"You behave yourself," said Mrs. Quimby, and meant it.

Ramona made sure she answered the door-bell when the guests arrived. There they stood—Aunt Bea and Uncle Hobart.

"Good evening, Ramona." Uncle Hobart, who had grown a neat beard and was wearing a jacket and tie, spoke to Ramona as if they were the same age.

Ramona was blunt. "Mr. Kemp, how come

you're still here?" Nobody would catch her calling him Uncle Hobart even though, because of Howie, this was the way she thought of him.

"Ramona!" Mrs. Quimby's voice was a warning. "Come on in," she said to the couple. "Don't pay any attention to Ramona."

Aunt Bea laughed and said to Ramona, "Hobart and I have renewed our high school friendship."

"Does he still spit?" Ramona asked under her breath, hoping her mother wouldn't hear.

"Not on the carpet," answered Uncle Hobart under his breath.

Mrs. Quimby had heard. "Ramona, do you want to go to your room?"

"No." Ramona sulked. Aunt Bea would be sorry if the family moved off to the land of sheep. Where would she go for Thanksgiving and Christmas? Her imagination spun a sad picture of Aunt Bea alone in her apartment, eating a frozen chicken pie.

When dinner was served, Ramona was seated

across from Uncle Hobart. While the adults talked and laughed, she stared at her plate until a lull came in the conversation, when she asked as politely as she could under the circumstances, "Mr. Kemp, I expect you'll be going back to Saudi Arabia soon."

He smiled a very nice smile. "What's the matter, Ramona? Are you trying to get rid of me?"

Ramona looked down at her plate.

"As a matter of fact, I'm not going to Saudi Arabia at all," Uncle Hobart informed Ramona. "I'm going to Alaska."

At least he was going someplace.

"That's why I grew a beard," he explained. "Alaska is cold in winter and full of mosquitoes in summer."

"Oh," said Ramona.

"Of course, women can't grow beards, so they scratch a lot in summer," said Uncle Hobart.

Ramona refused to laugh.

When dessert had been eaten by everyone

102

except Mrs. Quimby, who was careful about calories, and the adults were drinking coffee, Ramona was about to ask to be excused when Uncle Hobart spoke directly to her. "Ramona," he said, "how would you like to have me for an uncle?"

Ramona felt her face grow red. She was surprised and puzzled by his question. She wanted to say, No, thank you. Of course, grown-ups would think her rude, so she said, "You're already Howie and Willa Jean's uncle."

"I would like to have a couple of ready-made nieces," said Uncle Hobart.

Ramona had not caught on. "But how could you be our uncle?" she asked.

"Nothing to it," said Uncle Hobart. "All I have to do is marry your Aunt Beatrice."

Ramona sank back in her chair and thought, How dumb can I get? Aunt Bea was trying to hide her laughter, which did not make Ramona feel any better.

"You mean—" began Beezus.

Aunt Bea burst out laughing. "Hobart and I

103

are getting married in two weeks, before we leave for Alaska. There is oil in Alaska, too, you know."

Ramona frowned at Uncle Hobart. Why didn't he come right out and say he and Aunt Bea were going to marry? Her parents were smiling. They already knew and hadn't said a word. Traitors! Ramona felt as if her world were falling apart—Aunt Bea in Alaska, the Quimbys among strangers, sagebrush, and sheep.

"But Aunt Bea, what will you do in Alaska?" asked Beezus.

"Fish through the ice," said Uncle Hobart. "Build us an igloo."

"Don't listen to him," said Aunt Bea. "I plan to teach. I sent off an application and received a telegram accepting me."

Suddenly Ramona saw the solution to all her family's problems. "Aunt Bea," she said, bursting with excitement. "If you aren't going to teach in Portland, Daddy can have your job."

Sudden silence at the table. "I'm afraid not," said Aunt Bea gently. "I'm not going to be replaced. My school is not expecting as many pupils next fall and is not hiring any teachers."

"Oh," said Ramona. There was nothing more to say. Her happy plan had come to nothing.

The silence was broken by Beezus. "Oh, Aunt Bea!" She was ecstatic. "A wedding!"

"We aren't planning a wedding," said Aunt Bea. "There isn't time. We're going to be married at the City Hall."

"Bea, you can't." Mrs. Quimby was distressed. "A wedding should be a happy occasion, a gift from the bride's family."

"But there isn't time for a real wedding," insisted Aunt Bea. "Dad can't plan a wedding from his mobile home in Southern California. With a baby due so soon, you can't possibly take on a wedding."

"Aunt Bea," wailed Beezus. "There must be a way. It isn't fair for Mom to have had a wedding and you to get married at City Hall without any bridesmaids or anything."

Mrs. Quimby's voice was gentle. "Don't forget—your Grandma Day was living when I was married. She arranged it all."

"Don't men count in this event?" asked Uncle Hobart. "I don't like the idea of a City Hall wedding myself. There's no reason why we can't throw together some kind of wedding."

Pooh to you, thought Ramona with a scowl. You'd just mess things up.

"But weddings aren't that simple." Mrs. Quimby pushed her chair back from the table to rest her arms on the bulge that was Algie. "You can't throw together a wedding."

"Nonsense," said Uncle Hobart. "Women just make them complicated. Watch me take charge."

"You could wear Mother's wedding dress," Beezus suggested to her aunt. She and Ramona had often lifted their mother's wedding dress from its tissue-paper-lined box to admire. Beezus always held it up and tried on the veil in front of the mirror.

"There you are," said Uncle Hobart. "The wedding dress is taken care of."

"But you won't catch me being matron of honor, not in my shape," said Mrs. Quimby.

"Beezus and Ramona can be bridesmaids,

and I won't have a matron of honor." Aunt Beatrice was beginning to like the new plan.

Ramona perked up at the thought of being a bridesmaid. A wedding might be interesting after all.

"Willa Jean can be a flower girl." Aunt Bea stopped and frowned. "Oh, what am I thinking about? I have to write out performance reports for twenty-nine third-graders, we both have to buy cold weather clothes for Alaskan winters, I have to sell my car, Hobart has to trade in the van on a four-wheel-drive truck, and—"

"You have a great new ski outfit," interrupted Uncle Hobart, who probably did not know that a man named Michael had been the reason for the ski clothes. Whatever happened to Michael? Only Aunt Bea knew.

Uncle Hobart went on. "And all you have to write on those twenty-nine performance reports is, 'You have a great kid who will turn out okay.' That's what parents want to hear, and most of the time it's true."

Ramona looked at Uncle Hobart with real

respect. He understood about performance reports. Perhaps he would not make such a bad uncle after all.

Mr. Quimby, who had been quiet, spoke up. "I'll donate my frozen-food warehouse socks to cut down on shopping. As soon as school is out, I am leaving the frozen-food warehouse forever. The temperature in there is about the same as Alaska in winter, and you are welcome to my socks. If the market hadn't furnished the rest of my cold-weather gear, I'd give that to you, too."

This news produced silence, broken by Ramona. "Daddy, did you hear from another school that wants you to teach?"

"No, Baby, I didn't," he confessed, "but I was offered a job managing one of the Shop-rite markets. The pay and fringe benefits are good. I accepted, and start as soon as school is out."

"Daddy!" cried Beezus. "You mean you're going back to that market and won't teach art after all? But you don't like working in the market."

"We can't always do what we want in life," answered her father, "so we do the best we can."

"That's right," said Mrs. Quimby. "We do the best we can."

"It's not the end of the world, Beezus. Being manager is better than being a checker and much better than filling orders in the frozen-food warehouse." Mr. Quimby's smile could not hide the discouraged look in his eyes. "Now let's get on with plans for the wedding."

Relief flowed through Ramona. No strange child would mark her walls with crayons. She would not have to leave Howie, her school, her friends. Only Aunt Bea would be missing.

Uncle Hobart broke the silence that followed Mr. Quimby's news by saying, "Yes, about our wedding. Women get all worked up and exhausted when there's a wedding in the family, but not this time. You invite your friends by telephone, and I'll take care of the rest. There's nothing to it."

110

The adult sisters looked at one another with amused "he'll-see" smiles. "Great!" said Aunt Bea. "I'll be perfectly happy with any wedding you plan. Now all I have to do is persuade Dad to leave his shuffleboard, bingo, and sunshine and come up from Southern California to give me away." The family had seen little of Grandpa Day since he had retired and moved away from Oregon's rainy winters.

"He'll come," said Ramona, who loved her grandfather. "He's got to come."

"First thing Saturday morning," said Uncle Hobart, "I'll gather up you girls, along with Willa Jean, and we'll go shopping for your dresses while Bea dashes off those progress reports."

"It sounds like the fastest wedding in the West," said Mr. Quimby.

Ramona and her sister exchanged a look that said each was wondering what shopping with a bachelor petroleum engineer would be like.

SEVEN

The Chain of Command

Saturday morning, Willa Jean and a very cross-looking Howie arrived with Uncle Hobart in his van to collect Beezus and Ramona to go shopping for wedding clothes.

"How come you're going shopping with us?" Ramona demanded of Howie.

Howie did not answer Ramona, but instead complained to his uncle, "I've said a million times I don't want to be a ring bearer. I don't care what Grandma says. I'm too big. That stuff is for little kids. Carrying a ring on a pillow is dumb. Besides, it will fall off."

"I'm on your side, kid," said Uncle Hobart. "But let's humor your grandmother. She's busy making a fancy pillow for the ring, and says she will fasten the ring in place with a couple of loose stitches. And don't blame me if my favorite nephew's a big kid instead of a little kid."

"I'm not your favorite nephew," said Howie. "I'm your only nephew."

"You may have competition when Algie arrives," said Uncle Hobart. "Now, Beezus, where do we go for girl things?"

"Well . . . there's a bridal shop in the mall of the shopping center." Beezus was shy about directing Uncle Hobart. "But I'm not sure they have our sizes."

"Heigh ho, off we go!" Uncle Hobart backed his van out of the driveway and headed for the shopping center, where they found the parking lot crowded. "Now what we need is a chain of command," said Uncle Hobart when he had finally found a parking space. "I'll keep an eye on Beezus, who keeps an eye on Howie, who keeps an eye on Ramona, who watches out for Willa Jean. Each makes sure that the next person behaves and doesn't get lost."

"I don't need Beezus to keep an eye on me," grumbled Howie. "And Beezus always behaves." Willa Jean slipped her fingers into Ramona's hand, an act that Ramona found touching and made her feel protective, even though the little girl's fingers were sticky. The

chain of command proceeded into the mall, where they found the bridal shop filled with pale, floating dresses, wedding veils, and thin, floppy hats.

"Oh—" breathed Beezus.

"Yuck," said Howie.

The three-way mirror tempted Ramona to look at herself, but she resisted. She must set a good example for Willa Jean. Howie flopped down on a couch and scowled at his feet. The saleswoman looked as if she wished they would all go away.

"Bridesmaid dresses for two, and one flower-girl dress." Uncle Hobart sounded as casual as if he were ordering hamburgers.

Dresses were produced. Beezus and Ramona were bashful about spending so much of Uncle Hobart's money and were uncertain about choosing. Willa Jean was not. "I like that one," she said, pointing to a ruffled pink dress in her size.

"Okay, girls?" asked Uncle Hobart. The sis-

115

ters, who would have preferred yellow, nodded. The correct sizes for Beezus and Ramona, it turned out, would have to be ordered from other outlets in the chain of bridal shops. Yes, they would arrive in time for the wedding. The saleswoman promised. While Uncle Hobart paid for all three dresses, Ramona whispered to Willa Jean to sit beside Howie. Willa Jean actually minded.

Ramona slipped over for a glimpse of herself in the three-way mirror, which reflected her back and forth from every angle. She began to dance, to watch all the Ramonas. Obediently, they imitated her, dancing on and on into the distance, tinier and tinier until they could no longer be seen. Forever me, thought Ramona. I go on forever.

"Now, what about our ring bearer?" Uncle Hobart looked at Howie, who slid down on the couch and scowled.

Ramona was aware that the saleswoman eyed Howie as if he did not belong on her couch.

She danced on, twirling to make the myriad Ramonas twirl.

"To dress properly," said the saleswoman, "a boy in a wedding party should wear short pants, knee socks, a white shirt, and a jacket; but ring bearers are usually little boys. Four- or five-year-olds."

"See, what did I tell you?" Howie said to his uncle.

Uncle Hobart ignored his nephew. "Come, Beezus," he said, holding the box with Willa Jean's dress under his arm. As the next link she said, "Come on, Howie," who said, "Come on, Ramona," who said, "Come on, Willa Jean. Thank you for being such a good girl." Willa Jean beamed. The saleswoman looked happy to see them go.

Uncle Hobart led his chain of command to a boys' shop where, much against Howie's wishes, he bought short navy blue pants, a white shirt, and a pale blue jacket. "Everybody will make fun of me," said Howie. The salesman said the shop did not carry knee socks for boys.

Beezus felt responsible for Howie. "Girls' shops have knee socks," she suggested.

"You shut up," said Howie.

Uncle Hobart's good nature was not disturbed. "Shut up yourself," was his cheerful order as he led his troops into a girls' shop, where he bought a pair of navy blue knee socks for Howie. "Now, Beezus, what else do we need for a wedding?"

"Flowers," was the answer.

On the way to the florist, the shoppers came to a ski goods store that was having a sale. "Just what your aunt and I need," said Uncle Hobart, leading the way among the racks of ski clothing, where he quickly bought quilted down jackets for himself and his bride, waterproof pants, fur-lined gloves, heavy socks, and boots, all great bargains. Fortunately, Beezus knew her aunt's sizes.

"You don't suppose he would wear any of this stuff at the wedding, do you?" Ramona whispered to Beezus as she pulled a man-sized jacket off Willa Jean.

"Who knows?" said Beezus. There was no telling what Uncle Hobart might do.

The troops carried all the bags and boxes across the hot parking lot to the van. On the way back to the mall, Willa Jean, who spotted the ice-cream store that sold fifty-two flavors, told her uncle she needed an ice-cream cone. Uncle Hobart agreed that ice-cream cones were needed by all.

Inside the busy shop, customers had to take numbers and wait turns. Ramona, responsible for Willa Jean, who could not read, was faced with the embarrassing task of reading aloud the list of fifty-two flavors while all the customers listened. "Strawberry, German chocolate, vanilla, ginger-peachy, red-white-and-blueberry, black walnut, Mississippi mud, green bubble gum, baseball nut." Grimly, Ramona read on, skipping pistachio because she wasn't sure how to pronounce it, and stumbling over nectarine and macadamia nut. "Avocado (avocado ice cream?), fudge brownie—" She thought Uncle

Hobart's number would never come, but of course it did.

"Five double scoops of chocolate mandarin-orange dipped in nuts," was Uncle Hobart's order.

Double scoops with nuts. Beezus and Ramona were impressed.

As ice-cream cones were handed around and the group walked out into the sunbaked parking lot, Uncle Hobart said, "In the heat and dust of Saudi Arabia, I lay on my bunk at night listening to the wolves howl and longing for chocolate mandarin-orange double-scoop ice-cream cones dipped in nuts."

Ramona licked a drip of ice cream. "I thought you said you dreamed of your mother's apple pie."

"That too," said Uncle Hobart. "A man can have more than one dream in life."

"They don't have wolves in Saudi Arabia," said Howie.

"Okay, listening to camels howl." Uncle

Hobart led the way to a flower shop in the mall, where they were told they could not enter with ice-cream cones. This did not bother Uncle Hobart, who pulled a list from his pocket, stood in the doorway, and ordered one bouquet of white flowers for the bride, three wreaths of little flowers for girls—here he pointed to the girls—and two bridesmaids' bouquets, not too big. "What color?" he asked Beezus, and took a big bite of ice cream.

"Mostly pink, to go with our dresses," said Beezus, daintily nibbling into her ice cream instead of licking.

"Pink," ordered Uncle Hobart, "and a little bunch of flowers for the flower girl. We can't have a flower girl without flowers, can we, Willa Jean?" Willa Jean was too busy trying to keep ahead of her melting ice cream to answer. "And whatever one groom, one best man, and two ushers wear in their buttonholes. Oh, yes, and a flower for my ring bearer here."

"Aw, Uncle Hobart," grumbled Howie as his

uncle handed over a credit card to the astonished florist and gave the time the flowers were to be delivered to the Quimbys' address. Willa Jean's flowers and the men's flowers were to go to the Kemps'.

"Come on, troops, let's go home," said Uncle Hobart. "Like I told you. There's nothing to planning a wedding."

Ramona hoped the dresses really would arrive in time as she licked the ice cream running down her arm. She knew Beezus was wishing the same thing.

"Uncle Hobart, I don't think camels howl," said Howie. "I think they sort of snort." Anyone could see Howie had no interest in the wedding.

Beezus, who had managed to eat her cone neatly, asked, "What about the church and minister?" She could not entirely trust Howie's uncle to remember.

Uncle Hobart crunched the last bite of his cone. "All taken care of, along with the wedding ring and the caterer, who will supply the food. But thanks for keeping track. I might forget something."

He probably will, thought Ramona, and wished she had a three-way mirror in her room at home so that when her bridesmaid dress was delivered, she could watch herself twirling forever.

EIGHT

The Families Get Together

Life at the Quimby home soon became busy and confused. Mr. Quimby now went to work regularly every morning, but Aunt Bea, to save paying a whole month's rent on an apartment she would leave before the end of the month, had moved in with the Quimbys. She stored most of her belongings in the Quimbys' basement, and the rest she piled in Ramona's room to be packed for shipment to Alaska.

Ramona slept on the floor in Beezus's room

in the sleeping bag Beezus had taken to camp one summer. The telephone rang constantly—neighbors offering to help with the wedding, people inquiring about Aunt Bea's little sports car that she had advertised for sale, friends returning calls to say yes, they would be delighted to attend the wedding.

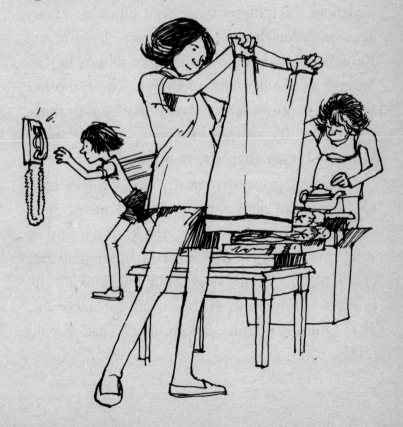

Teachers at Aunt Bea's school gave her a bridal shower. Most of the gifts were flat and easy to pack—bath towels, cheese boards, place mats. Aunt Bea's class gave her a coffee maker. Boxes piled up in Ramona's room.

Willa Jean's old bassinette was moved into the Quimbys' house and placed in the parents' bedroom. Neighbors gave Mrs. Quimby a baby shower, which meant more boxes. Beezus and Ramona hoped Algie would stay where he belonged until after the wedding. Their mother seemed to grow larger every day—or perhaps the maternity clothes she was wearing made her look bigger than she really was.

Wedding presents, mostly sets of bath towels, began to arrive. Ramona had never seen such beautiful towels—big, thick, fluffy, and in soft, pretty colors. She stroked them, laid her cheek against them, traced her finger along the designs. They were truly towels to marry for. The Quimbys' thin, faded towels had frayed edges.

The afternoon before the wedding rehearsal, Grandpa Day was arriving by plane so he could practice giving the bride away. Aunt Bea, whose car had been sold, borrowed Uncle Hobart's van, and with her nieces, drove to the airport to meet her father. Grandpa Day seemed older and thinner than the girls had remembered. He hugged his granddaughters, said they had grown, and announced he wanted to stay in a motel—no couch in a living room for him with a bunch of women fussing about a wedding. "At my age, I need a little peace and quiet," he informed his daughters. Leaving his carryon bag at the nearest motel, Aunt Bea drove her father to the Quimbys', where more boxes had arrived, none of them containing the bridesmaid dresses. "You can count on it," said Grandpa Day. "Something always goes wrong when there's a wedding." The sisters exchanged looks of anguish.

Uncle Hobart walked over to the Quimbys' to see the newest wedding presents—loot, he called them—and to pick up his van, which he was about to trade in on a four-wheel-drive truck for Alaska. A snowplow could be attached to the front.

Mrs. Quimby, looking tired and very big around the middle, was preparing a huge tossed salad because the two families were getting together before the rehearsal. Beezus was buttering stacks of French bread. Mr. Quimby arrived home late from work because a checker at the market had caught a shoplifter; the police had to be called, and questions answered. Even Aunt Bea looked tired.

When Uncle Hobart returned, desperate Beezus whispered to him that the bridesmaid dresses had not been delivered. "We'll see about that," he said and telephoned the shop, which promised the dresses first thing in the morning. "This evening. You will deliver those dresses this evening," ordered Uncle Hobart, as if he were speaking to a crew in the oil fields.

The Kemps arrived with two casseroles and

dessert. Because the dining room was too small to seat so many people, the food was set out on the dining room table. Everyone picked up a plate and helped himself. Ramona was happy that she was no longer responsible for Willa Jean, who had trouble serving herself and was helped by her grandmother.

When everyone was seated in the living room enjoying chicken with noodles, a casserole of mixed vegetables, and salad, Aunt Bea, sitting on the floor beside Uncle Hobart, asked, "What kind of flowers did you order for the church and reception hall?"

Uncle Hobart dropped his fork and slapped his forehead with his palm. "Flowers for the church! I completely forgot."

"Hobart, you didn't! I had them on the list." Aunt Bea was not sure he meant what he said. Her groom was a great kidder.

"I did," confessed Uncle Hobart. "We were all so busy eating ice-cream cones. I'll call the florist the first thing in the morning."

"Are you crazy?" cried Aunt Bea. "The day of the wedding, when florists are swamped with June weddings? Where would they find more flowers, especially so soon after the Rose Festival?" Worn out from progress reports, moving, and excitement, she turned to her fiancé and said, "I thought you said there was nothing to planning a wedding. Well, that just shows how wrong you can be."

"If I can be so wrong, why are you marrying me?" demanded Uncle Hobart. He looked tense, which was unusual for him.

Both families tried to act as if they were not listening—except, of course, the older children, who were fascinated. Willa Jean looked as if she might cry.

"That's a good question," said Aunt Bea.

"That's a good question! That's a good question! All the years I was in school, teachers were always telling me I had asked a good question. Half the time they didn't even answer. They just asked me what I thought the

answer should be, or asked some other kid to answer. Now you're telling me I asked a good question. You sound just like a teacher."

"I am a teacher." Aunt Bea's voice was cold.

Beezus and Ramona exchanged a "there-goes-the-wedding" look. Now the bridesmaid dresses no longer mattered. Howie looked hopeful, as if he thought he might escape carrying that ring on the pillow after all.

Uncle Hobart raised his voice. "Just once I

would like to hear a teacher answer a question. Why are you marrying me—if you still plan to marry me?"

Aunt Bea began by sounding like a teacher. "Hobart has asked a good question," she said with a pleasant smile before she turned and shouted, "Because I love you, you cootie!" She then burst into tears.

Ramona was stunned. Third- and fourth-graders called people cooties. Grown-ups did not.

Mr. Quimby put his arms around his wife, who looked as if she wished everyone would go away. "Feeling okay?" he whispered.

"I feel great." Mrs. Quimby's voice was unusually sharp. "Why shouldn't I feel okay when I'm having a baby? It's all perfectly natural. Stop fussing." Mr. Quimby looked hurt.

Uncle Hobart calmed down and looked ashamed. Aunt Bea wiped her eyes on the corner of one of her new bath towels.

"Why can't we just pick some flowers?" asked Ramona.

"What flowers?" demanded Beezus. "Those buggy pansies in the backyard?"

"Now, now," said Grandpa Day. "Just a case of pre-wedding jitters. Relax, everybody. I lived in this neighborhood for forty years, and I know how the women enjoy a challenge. Make a few phone calls, and you will have all the flowers you need."

Grandpa Day was right. Two neighbors had peonies in bloom, bushels of them; several had bumper crops of roses they would be happy to share. Another had plenty of laurel, which made a nice background and needed pruning anyway.

When the matter of the flowers was settled, Aunt Bea said with a wicked smile, "I forgot something, too. I forgot to tell you that I had invited all my third-graders. They wanted so much to come."

Oh, no, thought Ramona. Third-graders would gobble up all the food at the wedding reception and run around bumping into people and spilling things. Still, she looked forward to seeing the class she had heard so much about from Aunt Bea.

"Great!" said Uncle Hobart. "I'll order champagne for twenty-nine more guests."

Ramona was horrified. Twenty-nine third-graders sloshing around with champagne.

"Hobart!" Mrs. Kemp spoke severely to her youngest son. "Settle down and do be sensible. You can't serve champagne to children. Order some punch for them."

"Sure, Mom." Uncle Hobart glanced at his watch. "Speaking of forgetting, let's not forget the rehearsal."

The members of the wedding party whisked their dishes into the kitchen—they would eat Mrs. Kemp's homemade cheesecake later—then they climbed into the truck and the Kemps' car to go to the church. Ramona, Beezus, and Howie squeezed into the truck with Uncle Hobart and his bride. This was their only chance to ride in it.

"Swell, just swell," muttered Howie. "Twenty-nine kids laughing at me in girls' socks carrying a stupid little pillow."

"The dresses still haven't come," worried Beezus.

Uncle Hobart was reassuring. "Don't worry. You girls would look pretty even if you had to walk down the aisle in gym suits."

As the truck pulled away from the curb, a car pulled up. A man jumped out with a big box and ran up the Quimbys' driveway. Ramona glimpsed the word BRIDAL on the box. "Our dresses!" she shrieked.

"Whew, what a relief," said Beezus. "Now, if they will just fit."

"Uncle Hobart," said Howie, "you never did say what kind of noise a camel makes." Ramona wished Howie would forget about camels and pay attention to the wedding.

Uncle Hobart whinnied like a horse. "How's that?"

"I'm not sure it's right," said Howie.

Ramona, who was not worried about the fit

of her dress—safety pins could take care of that—or the sound of camels, wondered if twenty-nine third-graders, now promoted to the fourth grade, would arrive at the wedding with banana stickers on their foreheads and if Algie would stay where he belonged until it was all over. July was coming closer every day.

NINE

Ramona Saves the Day

The day of the wedding!

The bridesmaids' dresses were too long. "Pins!" cried Aunt Bea. "Get me some pins!" Algie made kneeling on the floor too difficult for Mrs. Quimby.

While Aunt Bea pinned up the hems, two for each because the dresses came with matching slips, the girls tried to stand very still, but how could they? The florist had delivered flowers that they couldn't wait to see. The girls fidgeted. "Beezus, just baste up the hems," said Aunt Bea when she had pushed the last pin in place. "They'll hold until after the wedding." She hurried off to press the wedding dress.

With flushed cheeks, Beezus basted as fast as she could. Ramona did not trust her sister's stitches and reinforced her hem with Scotch tape.

Everyone's hair had to be washed; everyone had to take a shower. By Ramona's turn for a shower, all the hot water had been used. Why, oh why, did the youngest always have to be last?

Mr. Quimby, who was taking the afternoon off from the market, was delayed. Would he never come? But he did come, and Ramona was sure she heard him say a bad word when he turned on the shower.

Where was Grandpa Day? "Bob, weren't you supposed to pick up Dad?" Mrs. Quimby called through the bathroom door.

"He said he wasn't ready and not to worry. He would get here on his own," answered Mr. Quimby between splutters. The family busied itself doing nothing—picking up wedding presents, putting them down, fussing with their hair, making sandwiches no one felt like eating.

Time to dress! Aunt Bea disappeared into Ramona's room while the girls dressed in Beezus's room. Ramona pulled on white socks while Beezus tugged at panty hose. Pink slips slid over their heads, then the dresses, the prettiest they had ever owned. They shoved their feet into their best white slippers. Beezus brushed her shining hair and Ramona's, too.

Feeling like princesses, the girls went to show off to their mother, who said they looked lovely. Except for Algie, the girls had never seen their mother look so beautiful. She was wearing a soft, airy dress borrowed from a neighbor who had already had a baby. That dress had been passed around among the women of Klickitat Street for several years. "A neighborhood needs only one dress-up maternity dress," explained Mrs. Quimby.

And then Aunt Bea appeared in her sister's wedding dress and veil. "Oh, Aunt Bea," sighed Beezus, "you're beautiful." Ramona was too stunned to speak.

Mrs. Quimby kissed her sister and said, "I hope that dress will be as lucky for you as it has been for me."

Ramona began to have an uneasy feeling that she had outgrown her white slippers, which she had not worn for at least a year. She would have died rather than complain.

"Where on earth is Dad?" the anxious bride wanted to know. "I don't want to keep Hobart waiting at the church."

Yes, where was Grandpa Day? Everyone worried, everyone fussed. His motel was called. No, his room did not answer. More worrying until Ramona, posted at the window, screamed, "Look!" There was Grandpa Day, arriving in a long black limousine driven by a real chauffeur wearing a real chauffeur's cap, just like chauffeurs on television.

"Why, Dad," cried Aunt Bea. "You didn't have to rent—"

"Say no more," said Grandpa Day. "I want to give my youngest daughter away in style."

"Wow!" exclaimed Ramona, forgetting her shoes. "And we get to ride in it!" Wait till Aunt Bea's third—now fourth—graders saw this.

143

Mrs. Quimby lifted wreaths of tiny pink roses from the florist's box, anchored them firmly to her daughters' hair with bobby pins before she handed them their nosegays. Both girls inhaled the fragrance of their flowers. "Ah-h."

Aunt Bea lifted out her bouquet of white blossoms. "Come along," ordered Grandpa Day. "The groom might get tired of waiting and leave." The family climbed into the limousine, Mr. Quimby sitting with the chauffeur and

Beezus and Ramona sitting on fold-down seats facing the bride, their mother, and their grandfather. Under her long dress, Ramona slipped her feet out of her pinching slippers so she could enjoy every second of the ride.

"Now remember, girls," said Mrs. Quimby, "after you take your places at the front of the church, *stand still*."

As the limousine glided up to the church, Aunt Bea's class, arriving in car pools, was properly awed. They climbed quietly out of their ordinary cars and walked in pairs into the church. Most of the boys were wearing stiff new jeans and clean shirts. A couple wore suits. The girls were dressed in their best. Ramona could see that many heads of hair had been washed in Portland that morning and that Aunt Bea had instructed her class in wedding behavior. Then she discovered she had to squeeze hard to get her feet back into her shoes.

The wedding party entered a small room behind the church reception room, where all the

Kemps except Uncle Hobart and Howie's father, who was the best man, were waiting. Ramona was surprised to see how pretty Willa Jean looked with the wreath of roses resting on her fair curls. Howie leaned against the wall in his short pants and knee socks. Except for his grumpy expression, Ramona thought he actually looked handsome, until he began to sing, very, very softly:

> "*Here comes the bride,*
> *Fair, fat, and wide.*
> *Here comes the groom,*
> *Skinny as a broom.*
> *Here comes the usher,*
> *The old toilet-flusher.*"

"Howie, you shut up!" ordered Ramona with all the ferocity she could summon in a whisper. What if the bride heard? The bride did hear, and laughed. She knew what to expect from boys Howie's age. Mrs. Kemp handed her

146

grandson a small lace pillow with the wedding ring fastened in place with basting stitches.

"It will probably fall off," he predicted.

"No, it won't," said his grandmother. "I've made sure of that."

"Beezus, my feet are killing me," whispered Ramona with tears in her eyes. "My shoes are way too short."

"So are mine," agreed Beezus. "I'll never make it down the aisle."

Grandmother Kemp was lining up the wedding party in the order in which they were to enter the church. "Once you reach your place at the front of the church, *don't move*," she ordered.

"Quick," whispered Beezus to Ramona. "Give me your shoes." Astonished, Ramona obeyed. As the wedding party proceeded through the reception room to the vestibule of the church, Beezus dropped the two pairs of slippers into a large bouquet of rhododendron blossoms. When the organ burst forth with the processional, the girls stifled their giggles. Uncle Hobart's friends, the bearded ushers splendid in their rented clothes, grinned at the girls and, after escorting Howie's mother and grandmother and Mrs. Quimby to the front pew, returned to walk slowly down the aisle together.

Ramona and Beezus counted to four. With the carpet tickling the bottoms of their feet and their nosegays quivering from nervousness, they followed, slowly and with dignity. Ramona could hear Willa Jean counting to four, and knew that she was following, and behind her, four counts later, Howie. Uncle Hobart and Howie's father, surprisingly handsome, were waiting with the minister at the end of what seemed like a long, long aisle.

Suddenly all the guests rose to their feet. Aunt Bea, on the arm of her father, had entered the church. Her class strained for a glimpse of their teacher.

From her place at the front of the church, Ramona could see her aunt, almost floating on the arm of Grandpa Day. Then they, too, took their places. The ceremony began. Grandpa Day gaveth this woman, as the minister called Aunt Bea, to be married and stepped back to the front pew. So much for the father of the bride.

All went well, with Ramona happily wiggling her toes inside her socks, until Howie's father tried to lift the wedding ring from the pillow. Unfortunately, Howie's grandmother, not trusting her grandson, had fastened the ring with such tight stitches it would not lift. Mr. Kemp tugged. The ring remained in place. Howie clutched the pillow in a good tight grip while his father yanked. The ring came off the pillow, slipped through his fingers, flew through the air, and disappeared.

The guests gasped. The children in the wedding party, instructed not to move, stood like statues. The wedding had come to a standstill. The men in the party began to look around for the ring. Even Aunt Bea took a step back to see if it had rolled under her skirt. The men leaned forward, searching. In a minute, they might even be on their knees, feeling around on the carpet with their hands. Ramona prayed that Aunt Bea's class would not giggle.

Then, as Aunt Bea bent over, Ramona caught a glimpse of something shiny.

The wedding ring was around the heel of the bride's sandal. How did it get there? It must have rolled under Aunt Bea's dress, and when she stepped back, she stepped into it. A rustle went through the church, the sound of restless, uneasy guests. Something must be done, and now.

What should Ramona do? She was under strict orders not to move, but she was the only one who knew where the ring had landed. She thought fast. Why should she obey Mrs. Kemp, who had sewed the ring too tight and been the cause of its disappearance? In a minute someone would snicker and set off the whole congregation. Ramona could not bear to have her aunt's wedding laughed at. She decided to act, even if it meant showing her white socks. Laying her nosegay on the carpet, Ramona got down on her hands and knees, prayed her wreath wouldn't slip, crawled over to her aunt, reached under her skirt, took hold of her ankle, and when the surprised bride looked down, raised her foot and pulled the ring off her heel. Ramona then crawled backward, picked up her nosegay, handed the ring to the best man, and took her place once more, standing like a statue with her wreath still in place. Aunt Bea flashed Ramona a smile while her lips silently formed the words "thank you."

Everyone in the church relaxed, the wedding proceeded as if nothing had happened. Oh, that romantic moment when the minister pronounced the couple husband and wife, Uncle Hobart kissed Aunt Bea, and the organ sounded notes of joy! The wedding party sped up the aisle and into the reception hall where, under Howie's grandmother's direction, they formed a receiving line.

Guests trickled in, kissed the bride, congrat-
ulated the groom, and told Beezus and Ramona
they looked sweet, pretty, charming, and like
flowers—a new experience for Ramona. Some
said, "So this is the girl who saved the day," or
"It's a good thing you found the ring." One
said, "You were a real little heroine." Ramona
smiled modestly. One old gentleman told her
she looked "as pretty as a speckled pup." Ramona had never been so filled with joy.

Aunt Bea's class was shy about kissing the
bride, so the bride kissed every one of them.
Some said hi to Ramona; others told her they
had heard about her from Miss Day, or said it
was a good thing she found the ring. Some girls
wistfully told her they thought her dress was
pretty. Several boys said, "How come you're
not wearing shoes?" Ramona did not mind. She
was so happy she felt as if she could stand in
the receiving line forever, but of course it came
to an end, and when it did, Howie's grandmother actually thanked Ramona for finding the

ring, smiled a real smile, and told her she looked pretty.

Waiters passed trays of tiny sandwiches, punch, and champagne. Ramona noticed each member of her aunt's class was careful to take only two sandwiches, which showed Aunt Bea had told them how to behave. No one spilled punch; nobody threw up.

Ramona helped herself to three sandwiches. As a member of the wedding party, she felt she deserved them. Besides, she was hungry. As she nibbled to make the sandwiches last, she had an idea that she whispered to Beezus. "If we had some string, we could tie our slippers to the bumper of Uncle Hobart's truck. We can't wear them anymore."

Beezus, usually so proper, was delighted with the idea. "There must be some string someplace," she said.

"I'll ask Howie," said Ramona.

Howie, who was leaning against the wall stuffing himself with what Ramona considered more

than his share of sandwiches, and looking embarrassed because the girls from Aunt Bea's class
stared at him with admiration, liked the idea. "I
don't carry string in these pants," he said, "but I
bet I can find some." He began to ask around
among the boys from Aunt Bea's class, and sure
enough, string was found in several pockets.
When Ramona pulled the slippers from the flowers, she discovered she did not want to leave the
reception. Neither did Beezus. They liked being
paid compliments one after another, and Beezus
had noticed a boy her age looking at her as if he
wanted to talk to her. Besides, the bride was
about to cut the wedding cake.

"You do it." Ramona shoved the shoes at
Howie.

"Sure," agreed Howie, glad to escape. The
donors of the string went with him and, by the
time the cake was cut, returned looking pleased
with themselves and ready for their share of
cake.

Uncle Hobart, whom Ramona had been
avoiding because she felt ashamed that she had

not been nicer to him, cornered her. "I want to thank my new niece for saving the day by finding the ring," he said and kissed her. His beard was not as scratchy as she had expected.

"Thank you, Uncle Hobart," she said, shy about calling him uncle for the first time. "It's nice, sort of, having an uncle. And thank you for our dresses."

"You're welcome. And I like having another spunky niece." Uncle Hobart and Ramona were friends. Peace at last!

The bride threw her bouquet, aiming it, Ramona suspected, at Beezus, who caught it, which meant she would be the next bride. The newlyweds, both laughing, ran out to Uncle Hobart's truck in a shower of rice and birdseed and drove off. Two pairs of white slippers danced from the rear bumper. The wedding was over.

The Quimbys climbed into Grandpa Day's rented limousine and sank back into the rich upholstery with happy sighs. You could make teddy bears out of these seats, they are so soft and furry, thought Ramona.

"Funny about those white shoes on the back of the truck," remarked Mr. Quimby. "They look familiar."

The girls burst into giggles. "They hurt," confessed Ramona. "They were too tight."

Mrs. Quimby, resting her arms on Algie, smiled. "I had forgotten how long you girls had had those shoes," she said. "I should have thought."

Ramona marveled that neither of her parents said the girls should have saved Beezus's slippers for Ramona to grow into.

"I'm starved," announced Grandpa Day. "Giving away a bride is hard work, and that dainty little wedding food doesn't fill me up. When we get home, I'll send out for pizza."

Pizza! thought Ramona. A limousine and a pizza! The end of a perfect day.

TEN

Another Big Event

After the wedding, everyone felt let down, the way they always felt the day after Christmas, only worse. Nothing seemed interesting after so much excitement. Grandpa Day had flown back to his sunshine and shuffleboard. Mr. Quimby was at work all day. Friends had gone off to camp, to the mountains, or the beach. Howie and Willa Jean had gone to visit their other grandmother.

"Girls, please stop moping around," said Mrs. Quimby.

"We can't find anything to do," said Beezus.

Ramona was silent. If she complained, her mother would tell her to clean out her closet.

"Read a book," said Mrs. Quimby. "Both of you, read a book."

"I've read all my books a million times," said Ramona, who usually enjoyed rereading her favorites.

"Then go to the library." Mrs. Quimby was beginning to sound irritable.

"It's too hot," complained Ramona.

Mrs. Quimby glanced at her watch.

"Mother, are you expecting someone?" asked Ramona. "You keep looking at your watch."

"I certainly am," said her mother. "A stranger." With a big sigh, Mrs. Quimby sank heavily to the couch, glanced at her watch again, and closed her eyes. The girls exchanged guilty looks. Their poor mother, worn out by Algie kicking her when there was so much of her to feel hot.

"Mother, are you all right?" Beezus sounded worried.

"I'm fine," snapped Mrs. Quimby, which surprised the girls into behaving.

That evening, the sisters helped their mother put together a cold supper of tuna fish salad and sliced tomatoes. While the family was eating, Mr. Quimby told them that now that the "Hawaiian Holidays" sale with bargains in fresh pineapple and papaya had come to an end, all the Shop-rite markets were preparing for "Western Bar-b-q Week" with specials on steak, baked beans, tomato sauce, and chili. He planned to paint bucking broncos on the front windows.

Mrs. Quimby nibbled at her salad and glanced at her watch.

"And everybody will see your paintings," said Ramona, happy that her father was now an artist as well as a market manager.

"Not quite the same as an exhibit in a museum," said Mr. Quimby, who did not sound as happy as Ramona expected.

Mrs. Quimby pushed her chair farther from the table and glanced at her watch. All eyes were on her.

162

"Shall I call the doctor?" asked Mr. Quimby.

"Please," said Mrs. Quimby as she rose from the table, hugged Algie, and breathed, "Oo-oo."

Ramona and Beezus, excited and frightened, looked at one another. At last! The fifth Quimby would soon be here. Nothing would be the same again, ever. Mr. Quimby reported that the doctor would meet them at the hospital. Without being asked, Beezus ran for the bag her mother had packed several weeks ago.

Mrs. Quimby kissed her daughters. "Don't look so frightened," she said. "Everything is going to be all right. Be good girls, and Daddy will be home as soon as he can." She bent forward and hugged Algie again.

The house suddenly seemed empty. The girls listened to the car back out of the driveway. The sound of the motor became lost in traffic.

"Well," said Beezus, "I suppose we might as well do the dishes."

"I suppose so." Ramona tested all the doors, including the door to the basement, to make sure they were locked.

"Too bad Picky-picky isn't here to eat all this tuna salad no one felt like eating." Beezus scraped the plates into the garbage.

To her own surprise, Ramona burst into tears and buried her face in a dish towel. "I just want Mother to come home," she wept.

Beezus wiped her soapy hands on the seat of her cutoff jeans. Then she put her arms around

Ramona, something she had never done before. "Don't worry, Ramona. Everything will be all right. Mother said so, and I remember when you came."

Ramona felt better. A big sister could be a comfort if she wanted to.

"You got born and Mother was fine." Beezus handed Ramona a clean dish towel.

Minutes crawled by. The long Oregon dusk turned into night. The girls turned on the television set to a program about people in a hospital, running, shouting, giving orders. Quickly they turned it off. "I hope Aunt Bea and Uncle Hobart are all right," said Ramona. The girls longed for their loving aunt, who was cheerful in times of trouble and who was always there when the family needed her. Now she was in a truck, riding along the Canadian Highway to Alaska. Ramona thought about bears, mean bears. She wondered if two pairs of white shoes still danced from the bumper of the truck.

The ring of the telephone made Ramona feel

as if arrows of electricity had shot through her stomach as Beezus ran to answer.

"Oh." There was disappointment in Beezus's voice. "All right, Daddy. No. No, we don't mind." When the conversation ended, she turned to Ramona, who was wild for news, and said, "Algie is taking his time. Daddy wants to stay with Mom and wanted to be sure we didn't mind staying alone. I said we didn't, and he said we were brave girls."

"Oh," said Ramona, who longed for her father's return. "Well, I'm brave, I guess." Even though the evening was unusually warm, she closed all the windows.

"I suppose we should go to bed," said Beezus. "If you want, you can get in bed with me."

"We better leave lights on for Daddy." Ramona turned on the porch light, as well as all the lights in the living room and hall, before she climbed into her sister's bed. "So Daddy won't fall over anything," she explained.

"Good idea," agreed Beezus. Each sister knew the other felt safer with the lights on.

"I hope Algie will hurry," said Ramona.

"So do I," agreed Beezus.

The girls slept lightly until the sound of a key in the door awoke them. "Daddy?" Beezus called out.

"Yes." Mr. Quimby came down the hall to the door of Beezus's room. "Great news. Roberta Day Quimby, six pounds, four ounces, arrived safe and sound. Your mother is fine."

Barely awake, Ramona asked, "Who's Roberta?"

"Your new sister," answered her father, "and my namesake."

"*Sister*." Now Ramona was wide-awake. The family had referred to the baby as Algie so long she had assumed that of course she would have a brother.

"Yes, a beautiful little sister," said her father. "Now, go back to sleep. It's four o'clock in the morning, and I've got to get up at seven-thirty."

The next morning, Mr. Quimby overslept and ate his breakfast standing up. He was halfway out the door when he called back, "When I get off work, we'll have dinner at the Whopperburger, and then we'll all go see Roberta and your mother."

The day was long and lonely. Even a swimming lesson at the park and a trip to the library did little to make time pass. "I wonder what Roberta looks like?" said Beezus.

"And whose room she will share when she

outgrows the bassinette?" worried Ramona.

The one happy moment in the day for the girls was a telephone call from their mother, who reported that Roberta was a beautiful, healthy little sister. She couldn't wait to bring her home, and she was proud of her daughters for being so good about staying alone. This pleased Beezus and Ramona so much they ran the vacuum cleaner and dusted, which made time pass faster until their father, looking exhausted, came home to take them out for hamburgers and a visit to the fifth Quimby.

Ramona could feel her heart pounding as she finally climbed the steps to the hospital. Visitors, some carrying flowers and others looking careworn, walked toward the elevators. Nurses hurried, a doctor was paged over the loudspeaker. Ramona could scarcely bear her own excitement. The rising of the elevator made her stomach feel as if it had stayed behind on the first floor. When the elevator stopped, Mr. Quimby led the way down the hall.

"Excuse me," called a nurse.

Surprised, the family stopped and turned.

"Children under twelve are not allowed to visit the maternity ward," said the nurse. "Little girl, you will have to go down and wait in the lobby."

"Why is that?" asked Mr. Quimby.

"Children under twelve might have contagious diseases," explained the nurse. "We have to protect the babies."

"I'm sorry, Ramona," said Mr. Quimby. "I didn't know. I am afraid you will have to do as the nurse says."

"Does she mean I'm *germy*?" Ramona was humiliated. "I took a shower this morning and washed my hands at the Whopperburger so I would be extra clean."

"Sometimes children are coming down with something and don't know it," explained Mr. Quimby. "Now, be a big girl and go downstairs and wait for us."

Ramona's eyes filled with tears of disappointment, but she found some pleasure in riding in the elevator alone. By the time she reached the lobby, she felt worse. The nurse called her a little girl. Her father called her a big girl. What was she? A germy girl.

Ramona sat gingerly on the edge of a Naugahyde couch. If she leaned back, she might get germs on it, or it might get germs on her. She swallowed hard. Was her throat a little bit sore? She thought maybe it was, way down in back. She put her hand to her forehead the way her mother did when she thought Ramona might have a fever. Her forehead was warm, maybe too warm.

As Ramona waited, she began to itch the way she itched when she had chickenpox. Her head itched, her back itched, her legs itched. Ramona scratched. A woman sat down on the couch, looked at Ramona, got up, and moved to another couch.

Ramona felt worse. She itched more and scratched harder. She swallowed often to see how her sore throat was coming along. She

peeked down the neck of her blouse to see if she might have a rash and was surprised that she did not. She sniffed from time to time to see if she had a runny nose.

Now Ramona was angry. It would serve everybody right if she came down with some horrible disease, right there in their old hospital. That would show everybody how germfree the place was. Ramona squirmed and gave that hard-to-reach place between her shoulder blades a good hard scratch. Then she scratched her head with both hands. People stopped to stare.

A man in a white coat, with a stethoscope hanging out of his pocket, came hurrying through the lobby, glanced at Ramona, stopped, and took a good look at her. "How do you feel?" he asked.

"Awful," she admitted. "A nurse said I was too germy to go see my mother and new sister, but I think I caught some disease right here."

"I see," said the doctor. "Open your mouth and say 'ah.'"

Ramona *ahhed* until she gagged.

"Mh-hm," murmured the doctor. He looked so serious Ramona was alarmed. Then he pulled out his stethoscope and listened to her front and back, thumping as he did so. What was he hearing? Was there something wrong with her insides? Why didn't her father come?

The doctor nodded as if his worst suspicions had been confirmed. "Just as I thought," he said, pulling out his prescription pad.

Medicine, ugh. Ramona's twitching stopped. Her nose and throat felt fine. "I feel much better," she assured the doctor as she eyed that prescription pad with distrust.

"An acute case of siblingitis. Not at all unusual around here, but it shouldn't last long." He tore off the prescription he had written, instructed Ramona to give it to her father, and hurried on down the hall.

Ramona could not remember the name of her illness. She tried to read the doctor's scribbly cursive writing, but she could not. She could only read neat cursive, the sort her teacher wrote on the blackboard.

Itching again, she was still staring at the slip of paper when Mr. Quimby and Beezus stepped out of the elevator. "Roberta is so tiny." Beezus was radiant with joy. "And she is perfectly darling. She has a little round nose and—oh, when you see her, you'll love her."

"I'm sick." Ramona tried to sound pitiful. "I've got something awful. A doctor said so."

Beezus paid no attention. "And Roberta has brown hair—"

Mr. Quimby interrupted. "What's this all about, Ramona?"

"A doctor said I had something, some kind of *itis*, and I have to have this right away." She handed her father her prescription and scratched one shoulder. "If I don't, I might get sicker."

Mr. Quimby read the scribbly cursive, and then he did a strange thing. He lifted Ramona and gave her a big hug and a kiss, right there in the lobby. The itching stopped. Ramona felt much better. "You have acute siblingitis," explained her father. "*Itis* means inflammation."

Ramona already knew the meaning of sibling. Since her father had studied to be a teacher, brothers and sisters had become siblings to him.

"He understood you were worried and angry because you weren't allowed to see your new sibling, and prescribed attention," explained Mr. Quimby. "Now let's all go buy ice-cream cones before I fall asleep standing up."

Beezus said Roberta was too darling to be called a dumb word like sibling. Ramona felt silly, but she also felt better.

For the next three nights, Ramona took a book to the hospital and sat in the lobby, not reading, but sulking about the injustice of having to wait to see the strange new Roberta.

On the fourth day, Mr. Quimby took an hour off from the Shop-rite Market, picked up Beezus and Ramona, who were waiting in clean clothes, and drove to the hospital to bring home his wife and new daughter.

Ramona moved closer to Beezus when she saw her mother, holding a pink bundle, emerge from the elevator in a wheelchair pushed by a nurse and followed by Mr. Quimby carrying her bag. "Can't Mother walk?" she whispered.

"Of course she can walk," answered Beezus. "The hospital wants to make sure people get out without falling down and suing for a million dollars."

Mrs. Quimby waved to the girls. Roberta's face was hidden by a corner of a pink blanket, but the nurse had no time for a little girl eager to see a new baby. She pushed the wheelchair through the automatic door to the waiting car.

"*Now* can I see her?" begged Ramona when her mother and Roberta were settled in the front, and the girls had climbed into the back-seat.

"Dear Heart, of course you may." Mrs. Quimby then spoke the most beautiful words Ramona had ever heard, "Oh, Ramona, how I've missed you," as she turned back the blanket.

Ramona, leaning over the front seat for her first glimpse of the new baby sister, tried to

177

hold her breath so she wouldn't breathe germs
on Roberta, who did not look at all like the picture on the cover of *A Name for Your Baby*.
Her face was bright pink, almost red, and her
hair, unlike the smooth pale hair of the baby on
the cover of the pamphlet, was dark and wild.

Ramona did not know what to say. She did not feel that words like darling or adorable fitted this baby.

"She looks exactly like you looked when you were born," Mrs. Quimby told Ramona.

"She does?" Ramona found this hard to believe. She could not imagine that she had once looked like this red, frowning little creature.

"Well, what do you think of your new sister?" asked Mr. Quimby.

"She's so—so *little*," Ramona answered truthfully.

Roberta opened her blue gray eyes.

"Mother!" cried Ramona. "She's cross-eyed."

Mrs. Quimby laughed. "All babies look cross-eyed sometimes. They outgrow it when they learn to focus." Sure enough, Roberta's eyes straightened out for a moment and then crossed again. She worked her mouth as if she didn't know what to do with it. She made little snuffling noises and lifted one arm as if she didn't know what it was for.

"Why does her nightie have those little pockets at the ends of the sleeves?" asked Ramona. "They cover up her hands."

"They keep her from scratching herself," explained Mrs. Quimby. "She's too little to understand that fingernails scratch."

Ramona sat back and buckled her seat belt. She had once looked like Roberta. Amazing! She had once been that tiny, but she had grown, her hair had calmed down when she remembered to comb it, and she had learned to use her eyes and hands. "You know what I think?" she asked and did not wait for an answer. "I think it is hard work to be a baby." Ramona spoke as if she had discovered something unknown to the rest of the world. With her words came unexpected love and sympathy for the tiny person in her mother's arms.

"I hadn't thought of it that way," said Mrs. Quimby, "but I think you're right."

"Growing up is hard work," said Mr. Quimby as he drove away from the hospital. "Sometimes being grown-up is hard work."

"I know," said Ramona and thought some more. She thought about loose teeth, real sore throats, quarrels, misunderstandings with her teachers, longing for a bicycle her family could not afford, worrying when her parents bickered, how terrible she had felt when she hurt Beezus's feelings without meaning to, and all the long afternoons when Mrs. Kemp looked after her until her mother came from work. She had survived it all. "Isn't it funny?" she remarked as her father steered the car into their driveway.

"Isn't what funny?" asked her mother.

"That I used to be little and funny-looking and cross-eyed like Roberta," said Ramona. "And now look at me. I'm wonderful me!"

"Except when you're blunderful you," said Beezus.

Ramona did not mind when her family, except Roberta, who was too little, laughed. "Yup, wonderful, blunderful me," she said and was happy. She was winning at growing up.